A QUESTION OF THYME

When Jen answers an advertisement to create a 1915 herb garden for a TV documentary, she expects it to get her out of a money hole, not to change her life . . . Borderline recluse Theo Grainger is scarred mentally and physically from an appalling fall seven years ago. Adjusting to the presence of a TV documentary team next door is one thing. Dealing with Jen Matlock, who helps people in trouble whether they want her to or not, is something else entirely . . .

JAN JONES

A QUESTION
OF THYME

Complete and Unabridged

LINFORD
Leicester

First published in Great Britain in 2017

First Linford Edition
published 2018

A catalogue record for this book is available
from the British Library.

ISBN 978–1–4448–3811–4

Published by
F. A. Thorpe (Publishing)
Anstey, Leicestershire

Set by Words & Graphics Ltd.
Anstey, Leicestershire
Printed and bound in Great Britain by
T. J. International Ltd., Padstow, Cornwall

This book is printed on acid-free paper

A Question of Thyme
is dedicated to
Carole Blake
Forever missed
Especially in the early morning,
and late at night and at all the
parties in between

1

One of the trials of being born into a family of high achievers is maintaining a pleasant smile when they introduce you to strangers.

Like today, for instance, when we had been summoned home en masse for lunch to meet Ewan's new fiancée and her parents.

'I'll just run through everyone, shall I?' said Mum to Clare's family, not waiting for a reply before relaying to the rest of us with bright satisfaction that Clare herself was a rare-books archivist with a doctorate in Early Music and that her father was a rural dean in the north west of England.

Ewan opened his mouth to head her off, but Mum steamed on regardless. It came from being a teacher.

'Ewan you already know of course. He's our eldest. He's a civil engineer with some very prestigious projects to his name. Anthony is the next oldest. He's a lawyer. I'm not allowed to tell you the names of his most important clients. This is his wife Gina, who runs an art gallery in London.'

There was a swallowed pause as Mum hastily edited out the usual bit about Gina having previously been married to Ewan. Pity. That part often served to take the heat off me.

'Our third son, Chris, is an architect,' she said, picking up the thread again. 'He specialises in the sympathetic restoration and enhancement of listed buildings. And last but not least, this is Jen, our youngest.'

I waited.

'Jen . . . Jen runs her own herb business.'

Well, that wasn't too bad. It was certainly better than the time Gina had introduced me to the rich deb she'd lined up for Chris with the immortal words, ' . . . and Jen grew nearly all the vegetables we're eating today.'

Clare's mother, who had been looking slightly glazed, sat up straight. 'You grow herbs? But that's splendid!' She beamed at me with what appeared to be genuine delight. 'What a piece of luck. Now then, my poor bay tree hates it where we are now. Have you got a hardy variety? What would you recommend? Do you do mail order? You must give me your card. Oooh, Shropshire, that's practically next door.'

'Mum takes three-quarters of the garden with her whenever Dad gets a new preferment,' explained Clare with tolerant resignation. 'It's astonishing how often things don't die.'

I already liked Clare a lot more than I'd ever liked Gina. She was easy to talk to, for one thing, and her mother was lovely. Leaving Mum to catechise Chris on his lack of permanent girlfriend ('After all, Chris, it won't be long before you're thirty, so it really is about time you stopped playing the field'), I settled down for a nice chat about the prevailing weather conditions in the deanery garden. We were just discussing cold-tolerant herbs when Ewan wandered over and sat on the arm of Clare's chair.

'What's this about the business, Jen?' he asked with a furrow of brotherly concern. 'Chris mentioned you were having problems with the lease. Do you need backup? Have you asked Anthony to check the terms of the contract?'

Oh, cheers, Chris. I glared at him. He returned a bland *Who, me?* look over Mum's head Chris was the closest to me in age and we'd always been a pair, much the same as Ewan and Anthony had been. That didn't give him the right to interfere. He hadn't been supposed to tell anyone I'd been handed an eviction order and that Wild About Herbs was going to have to move. The way the family radar was suddenly trained on me, he'd disregarded the confidentiality clause in pretty comprehensive style.

'It's okay, thanks. I'm coping,' I said.

'Oh, Jen, that bad?' Ewan's expression

became even more concerned.

I silently ground my teeth. It was ridiculous the way my family were unfailingly convinced I couldn't possibly manage by myself. There was no need for them to rally round and come over all protective. I hardly ever leapt impetuously into situations without thinking ahead these days. 'Don't worry, Ewan. I'll sort it out,' I said.

'Jen, love, it's what brothers are for. What's the point you putting up with us all these years if you don't use us when you need us?'

I huffed crossly. I knew exactly what was going to happen now. They'd all start looking for sites for me to rent, and one of them would be perfect and much too close to home, and I'd have to take it and be grateful — and before you knew it, I'd have lost my independence and be back in the family fold again.

'If only you weren't so far away,' murmured Mum right on cue, breaking off from haranguing Chris to turn and gaze ruminatively at me. Chris took the opportunity to dart over to the chair next to Granny and ask how she was doing. Trust him. Out of the firing line and impeccably occupied at the same time.

As it happened, my current base in Shropshire had been chosen precisely because it was over two hours away from Edgware. Any closer and Mum would have me coming here for meals every other day and running the garden patch at her school in my spare time. She was the worst offender in the keep-an-eye-on-Jen stakes, but I wasn't wholly convinced Chris's recent commission hadn't been accepted purely because it was only a twenty minutes drive from my business. I did love my family, honestly. It was just that they could be a bit suffocating. And, I realised hollowly, it was the summer holidays, so Mum would have plenty of time on her hands to go nursery-hunting for me. I was doomed.

I muttered something placatory and

reached for my satchel. I'd been running late when Chris arrived to collect me ('When aren't you?' he'd said, rolling his eyes and refusing to give me extra time) and he'd simply scooped everything up from the door-mat and thrown it into the passenger footwell after me.

'Excuse me,' I said. 'Chris was so eager to get here that I didn't have time to deal with my post. One of these might be an order.'

Three of the letters were indeed orders, because a lot of my mail-order customers either didn't trust the online system with their bank details or they'd never got to grips with the internet in the first place, but that wasn't what caught my eye. Chris had picked up the local paper along with the rest, and there at the bottom of the front page, outlined in a smudged black border, was an URGENT: WANTED advert that might have been written with me in mind.

'Back in a moment,' I said, hastening

upstairs with my phone in one hand and the paper in the other.

'I need someone who knows about herbs.'

The director of the MovingInk TV documentary — Bruce, I'd been told by his assistant — sounded impatient. I quelled my nerves and spoke firmly into the phone. 'That's me. Jen Matlock. I specialise in growing herbs and wild plants. I can supply plants, expertise, dried herbs, essential oils . . . the whole range.'

'And you believe in it all, yes?'

I looked askance at the phone. Why else would I be out in all weathers sowing, weeding, harvesting the herbs and then drying them, infusing, packing them up and posting off orders? The only reason I wasn't pacing the floor with worry every night about my livelihood being sold from under my feet was that I was too flaming tired *not* to sleep.

'I believe one hundred percent in my products,' I reassured him. It was a lot easier to be firm up here in the box room, with the bolt I'd installed when I was thirteen pulled across my relentlessly helpful family, than it was downstairs. I went on, 'I'm genuinely passionate about the ability of the living world to provide what we need. We *should* use natural remedies, as our forebears did, instead of depending on synthesised medicines and flavourings. And I say that as a doctor's daughter.'

There was a silence from the other end. Had I been too enthusiastic? The memory of my university professor crossing the campus to avoid me for a full two years after I'd overrun my allotted three minutes of Great Man time at a department get-together sprang to mind. I scanned the newspaper advert again. '*URGENT: WANTED! Herb garden and maintenance for WW1 country house drama documentary. Expert knowledge of herbs/wild plants & their uses (including medicinal) essential. Wansdale Manor.*

Start immediately. '

I had the plants they needed. I had the knowledge. I had day-to-day orders, but no significant ongoing commissions to speak of, and I could really, really do with the cash a TV contract would bring in. Finding a new plot of land for my nursery would be significantly easier with actual money in the bank.

Outside I heard the betraying creak of a floorboard. On the other end of the phone I heard Bruce tapping his teeth. 'How long would it take you to plant us a historically accurate herb patch on site, suitable for a 1915 country house? It needs to look as though it's been there for years.'

I thought rapidly. From what I knew of the making of TV documentaries, which was taken almost entirely from programmes about the making of TV documentaries, these people worked fast. 'Depending on the terrain and what I'd have to clear first, about a week. As I'm local, maintenance will be easy.'

'Cost?'

'For mature plants?' I told him a rough price for various sizes of herb garden and heard him scribbling on a piece of paper.

'Okay, tell me about . . . rosemary.'

With a sudden judder of my heart, I realised this was an interview. No time for nerves. *Go, Jen, go!* 'Rosemary? Originally from the Mediterranean, adds a nice English taste to food. Use the essential oil for stimulating aromatherapy. It can be massaged into the skin or burnt in an oil burner. Historically, rosemary water is a disinfectant, but you can also add sprigs to rinsing water to make hair and clothes smell nice. It keeps its fragrance well when dried. It's often claimed it aids memory retention, as well as being the symbol of remembrance.'

'Filming starts in two weeks. We've got the cast and the script. What I need from you is set dressing and expertise. Be at Wansdale Manor first thing tomorrow and start sorting out a herb

11

garden. Coralie will email you the contract.'

I was in. Just like that. Oh, the relief. On the other hand, the work ... I began to calculate when lunch might be over and Chris ready to drive back again. Wansdale rang a very faint bell in the back of my mind, but I couldn't spare the time to chase it. I had orders to fill as soon as I got home if I was going to spend the rest of this week making a credible herb bed.

★ ★ ★

The iron-studded oak door of Wansdale Manor swung inward, revealing pan-elled walls of dull chestnut and floorboards so dark as to be nearly black. A self-possessed young woman with expensive hair and a chic business suit stood in the doorway, framed incongruously in a patch of sunlight straight out of a Dutch interior. This must be Coralie Deverell, Bruce's assistant. We were about the same age, but I would never project a similar effortlessly efficient aura if I practised for the rest of my life. Today's look, admittedly, might have been improved if I'd had more than three hours' sleep.

'Jen Matlock,' I said. 'Wild About Herbs. I've come to build a herb patch.'

Dust circled the woman's designer heels as she moved. The manor had clearly not been lived in for some time. She widened a window on the tablet computer in her left hand and gave it a small, precise tap. She wasn't at all my idea of a TV industry person. I, on the other hand, appeared to be exactly what she expected of a gardener. Her gaze travelled past me to where my van was parked.

I turned to look. 'It's all right to leave it there, is it?' I said, managing to keep my face straight and my voice expressionless. The struggle was not because of my van, which was a perfectly serviceable third-hand Kangoo. It was because I'd parked in front of the most extraordinary garage I have ever seen. At least, I assumed it was a garage. It was separate from the main house. The ground floor had clearly started life as vaulted stables; then there was a perilously tall top-heavy upper level that seemed to consist of a collection of turrets cemented randomly together. The whole thing was surmounted by an enormous wrought-iron clock. It was ridiculously out of scale and made the half-timbered facade of Wansdale Manor look refreshingly plain.

'It's a folly,' remarked Coralie unnecessarily. 'You can park there for now. The majority of the trucks won't arrive until we start filming.' She turned back, dismissing the architectural failings of an earlier age. 'Bruce?' she said into thin air.

I was startled until I saw she'd tapped her tablet and had a slim earpiece nestling under the blonde streaks of hair. I also wore one; Mum had given it to me so I would never again have an excuse for not hearing the phone when I was working. But whereas mine was mostly tangled in my hair, Coralie looked as if she'd been born with hers. I'd bet good money her voice recognition system never misbehaved either.

'Bruce, Jen Herbs is here. Do you want her reaction to the garden for the EPK?'

Jen Herbs? EPK? I was going to have to get used to TV shorthand.

Coralie's face took on an intense, listening look, then she gave a nod and beckoned to me. 'Come through.'

I stepped inside. The hall was huge. I could easily imagine medieval barons holding feasts here, servitors bearing groaning platters, dogs lolling by the fire. Right now it held a somewhat hasty arrangement of Edwardian furniture, a team of cleaners in SparkleCastle tabards attacking the windows, and three people dressed in black setting up lights. At the back, a handsome, if dusty, staircase ascended to a panelled gallery. More voices floated down from above.

'Fran,' called Coralie, 'initial walk-round with Jen Herbs for the EPK.'

There she went again. What the heck

was an EPK? I was distracted from the question by the sight of a wiry older woman leaving the lights, hoisting a camera to her shoulder and following us. Following *me*. Pointing the camera at *me*. I had the plunging sensation of having stepped into a sinkhole way over my head. No one had said I'd be filmed myself.

'I, um . . . ' I began.

'Act naturally and say your thoughts aloud,' instructed Coralie. 'These bits of footage will go into the 'making of' sections in the programmes, or the special features on the video. It's far more authentic to film an EPK — oh, sorry, electronic press kit — as we go along.'

I managed a strangled squawk.

Coralie looked at me contemplatively, then turned right at the end of the hall, walked down a short passage and opened a door on the left. 'This way,' she said.

I followed her through the door. In a former age, this would have been a back sitting room for the young ladies of the house. Now it contained an assortment of tables, bookcases, packing crates, trays of papers and drifts of old photographs. It also had beautifully anachronistic French windows opening straight out on to a deep rear terrace running the whole width of the house. 'Oh, how lovely!' I said, charmed by the room's light, airy beauty.

Coralie inclined her head a fraction. 'We're calling it the research room. For several months we've been gathering everything we can find that might have a bearing on the history of the house and the era we're interested in. A lot of it has gone into the script, and now it's here for the actors and crew to look through so they can soak themselves in the period. Bruce believes in total immersion when it comes to any of his projects. It's one of the hallmarks of his work. This room won't usually be so untidy. We only got in at daybreak so everything has simply been dumped in rooms to be going on with. The tenants

17

have been . . . difficult.'

I made a sympathetic noise that she took for encouragement.

'Honestly, I'm just so cross,' she said, becoming human in a sudden rush. 'Nobody has been using the house for the last couple of months, but they refused to give us access. We've had to do all the pre-production offsite. It's made it very awkward. Bruce is a tremendously organic director. It's been terribly frustrating for him. That's one reason why we've set up the production office here in the manor instead of working from trucks outside. It is cheaper, of course, which is a definite consideration, what with other significant costs, but also Bruce believes it will be a shortcut to the whole team feeling more connected with the film if we walk the same rooms and glimpse the same views on a daily basis that our characters would have done. He really is rather marvellous.'

'Er, yes,' I said, taken aback. It was the first time I'd experienced a woman of my own age having a fully fledged crush on a bloke. 'Are you in charge of the budget as well, then?'

She looked surprised that I had to ask. 'Yes, of course. It leaves Bruce free to carry the whole project in his head. Nothing is more detrimental to a beautifully realised concept than being constantly distracted by petty day-to-day decisions on money.'

Or petty forward planning, presumably. Still, I'd signed the contract now. I wasn't going to jeopardise it by mentioning that most people, when faced with the need for a herb patch, would have thought to organise it rather more than a bare two weeks before it was needed. I looked around the room. The nearest bookcase contained a wild mixture of coffee table books, gazetteers, battered parish records and herbals. I had to mentally sit on my hands to stop myself rummaging. I was quite capable of spending hours browsing ancient plant compendiums and looking at plans of bygone gardens. I could see now that the overflowing trays of ephemera had simply been unloaded on to the tables and were waiting for someone, probably Coralie herself, to file them properly. I picked up a photo at random. It was of an old-fashioned hospital ward with starched nurses, two men in uniform, and patients sitting to attention in flannel pyjamas. As I moved the photo, I dislodged a letter from a Lady Mary Wansdale dated 1914, beginning, 'My dear Evelyn, such trials we have had here! Louise is determined to be stubborn!'

Coralie nodded at the photograph. 'Wansdale was used as an auxiliary hospital during the Great War. The daughter of the house helped with the nursing and married one of the wounded officers. It's a lovely story. That's what we're focusing on for the series, the change in social conditions and expectations between the pre-war and inter-war period. Lady Mary and Louise had quite different attitudes. You can tell that from Lady Mary's letters to her friend. You wonder, really, how they would have managed *without* the war to shake things up. We're going to cut between the actors who are playing out the story and a range of present-day experts who'll tell the viewers the background information on everything we see on screen. From you, for example, we need to know the sort of plants Louise would have found useful and how to make the poultices or oils or whatever. We know from her mother's letters that she worked in the garden and the stillroom as well as doing the nursing.' She rubbed her neck, absently rotating it. 'Look at what you like in here. If you need me, the production office is next door. Or I may be with Bruce. We'll be getting more furniture in relays from our lock-up all day. One thing about doing the Great War, you can pick up the set dressing for absolutely nothing. It costs more to hire the van than it does to fill it with furniture. The props team have been having a lovely time trotting around all the country house auctions they can find.'

'Right,' I said, hoping I didn't sound as bewildered as I felt.

Coralie seemed satisfied with my response. 'Let me know as soon as you've identified whereabouts in the garden you want to use. Don't go near the boundary railings or down to the river. Workmen are dismantling electric wires. Oh, and remember to act naturally.'

She vanished in a busy rattle of heels. I stared after her, processing my immediate concerns from amongst the flood of incomprehensible technical information. They wanted me to make WW1 poultices? That would be a challenge. I knew lots of creams and salves, but I'd need to read up on them to make sure I had the dates right. However, that could come later. My priority right now was to make the grounds of Wansdale Manor look as though a herb bed had been established here for the past twenty years. Followed silently and rather alarmingly by Fran, I hitched my satchel further up my shoulder and went through the French windows to investigate the garden.

2

As soon as I got outside I stopped, right there on the terrace, astounded and overwhelmed at the view. Nothing in the dense half-timbering of the manor or the over-the-top gothic embellishments on the stable had prepared me for the simple loveliness of the design of the Wansdale Manor garden. From the stone terrace where I was standing, with its lichen-etched amphora balustrade and its fat Greek urns at each corner, the beds fell away gently towards the river in a set of irregular arcs, first sweeping to the left, then to the right, like an ice skater's progress across a snowy lake. Just beautiful.

'Oh my,' I said, barely breathing. 'Oh my goodness, this is lovely.'

Even the setting was jewel-like. There was woodland on the far side of the property and a market garden with a barn, offices and the remains of a walled enclosure behind the boundary railings on this near side. Down at the bottom of the garden ran the teal-blue shimmer of a river. If you had asked me to draw something more perfect, I wouldn't have been able to.

Out of the corner of my eye, I saw Fran move to one side, her camera fixed on my face. Oh help. I rested my fingers against the rough stone coping for courage, then clearing my throat and speaking my thoughts aloud very self-consciously, I started down the central steps.

It was evident that at some time in its past the garden had been planned. The zigzag curves of the path were laid in old brick, but enough pockets of chamomile brushed my ankles to suggest that the path might have originally started life as a green fragrant ribbon running between the beds and widening out at the river below. I'd seen that done before. In the very olden days, a chamomile path would have been a lot cheaper to lay than expensive bricks.

I explained this out loud and had a tiny breathing space as Fran got a nice close-up of the chamomile. I looked around, calmer now that I was surrounded by plants. The bed at the top of the slope, nearest the house, was crammed with roses, loading the air with the heavy scent of an English summer. A glance showed me they were all modern, but underneath their perfume there were other scents weaving through. Lavender, for example. I could see a great bush of it further down. More than one variety, judging from dark purple flower spikes blending with dusty blue. That could be very useful as far as the programme was concerned.

I was lucky in another respect, as I said to Fran. The manor garden was south-facing, mimicking the Mediterranean, a perfect suntrap for herbs. The new herb patch I was to make would be quick to establish. Where would be best? I moved further down the path. Already warm, I absently twisted my hair (which Dad described as pre-Raphaelite and everyone else called a disaster) into the artisan headscarf I used to keep it out of the way whilst working. I heard Fran give a grunt of approval. And now as I descended there was pennyroyal intruding on the path, and a great stand of fennel, just bursting into growth.

Lavender, fennel, chamomile . . . sage too, and something with a peppery edge. Bubbles of excitement were rising up in me, popping against my skin. A lot of the herbs I would need to plant were already here. I pointed them out to the camera, conjecturing as to why I thought they were scattered around rather than growing tidily in one bed. They'd originally have been grown for the kitchen; had to have been. A house this size would have warranted a cook until at least the inter-war period. So at one stage in the manor's history there would have been a proper herb bed in the

grounds. These plants were in all likelihood the descendants of long-ago escapees.

I looked again around the garden,
filtering out the modern bedding and
trying to see any sort of plan or pattern
in what was left. There wasn't one
— not as far as kitchen use was
concerned, anyway. However, half way
down to the siren call of the river, I
glimpsed a shed, hidden under an
overhanging swathe of willow. More
willows grew down to the water's edge,
the green fronds forming a dense
curtain brushing an underlying tangle
of nettles and brambles. I frowned. I
was fairly sure only the bottom one
would have been original planting. The
rest would have crept up over the years,
rooting from broken branches or where
leaves touched the ground.

'Words,' prompted Fran.

'Sorry.' I walked towards the shed.
'These willows aren't period,' I said
aloud. 'Not because they aren't old
trees — they are — but because they
take too much light from the beds. One

or two would have been here and the bark used for treating fevers. Saplings would have been harvested for the withies, but if the owners stopped employing a full time gardener, there would be no one to check their growth.' The shed was miraculously undamaged by the marauding trees. It was very old, square rather than rectangular, solid, with curlicues and fancy carving on the eaves. It was a true potting shed and workshop, a million miles from the larchlap, self-assembly flat packs sold in garden centres by the hundred any time during the last fifty years. I lusted after it like no one's business. 'This would have been the gardener's shed,' I said. 'There certainly wouldn't have been any willows allowed so close to it originally because the gardener wouldn't have been able to see to work on anything inside.'

'Can't use it for filming,' commented Fran dispassionately. 'Not unless we take the front off.'

I glanced at her, half-horrified. I

expected her to be joking, but she appeared to be in earnest. I moved hurriedly away. I'd investigate the shed privately later.

Herbs. That was what I was here for. I picked my way towards the furry silver-green mound of sage in the centre of the plot. Behind it was rosemary, as sharp on the soft air as Sunday lunch. Perennial both of them, and like the lavender to one side with its gnarled woody stems, very old. I rubbed a sage leaf between my fingers and sniffed at the comforting scent, thinking about the WW1 photo I'd seen in the research room and Coralie's theory that this garden had supplied medicinal aid for the wounded men. Nothing was more likely, in my opinion. I wasn't sure that these present plants were a century old, but they could easily be cuttings of the originals. It would be nice to have a living link to the past.

I stirred the ground with my boot. This particular bed was too full of established roots to be suitable for infilling with new plants. The one below, however, just held scrappy ground cover. No one would miss that. I dropped down a level and hunkered down, pulling up clumps of vegetation and pushing aside dead, matted stems. They came away easily. The soil was poor, gritty between my fingers, ideal in a herb garden where nutrient poverty increases the strength of the flavour. I said as much aloud to Fran. It was easier to pretend I was talking to her rather than the camera.

I could smell marjoram. Looking towards the river as I sniffed the air, I also saw a bush of sweet cicely, a low growing patch of thyme and flashes of orange marigold. On the other side of the path, lush stems of nasturtium tumbled down the levels. I pursed my lips. Nothing cried out the lack of a permanent gardener like a riot of nasturtiums in a main flowerbed. Sure, they were glorious in late summer and early autumn, with their orange and yellow flowers pushing above the saucer leaves, but they were rank in winter and after a frost the pulpy morass stifled the growth of anything else until it was cleared. I reminded myself firmly that I was only here to make a herb patch, no matter how much I itched to bring the whole garden back to a productive life.

I applied myself to the job in hand. Probing through the hard, dry soil, my fingertips touched smooth brick. That was odd. I tugged at it, expecting it to be a fragment, but it wouldn't budge. I'd need my trowel to go further. I got up to return to the van.

'I'd like to use this bed,' I said to Fran, brushing down my jeans. 'I can clear it easily and it's got a nice defined shape. Will it be okay for you for filming?'

Fran lowered her camera and swept a professional eye around. 'Sure,' she said. 'I'll run what I've got by Bruce, then come back in half an hour and shoot a few minutes of you digging.'

I wasn't sure half an hour would

advance me as far as digging, but I could certainly make a start on clearing the ground. It occurred to me that the old shed might hold gardening tools. If MovingInk had hired the whole of the house and grounds, I could use what was there — provided they were in good condition — rather than bringing all my own equipment down from the van. Some of the tools in the shed might even be period. Gardeners rarely threw anything away. I went to look.

Under the shade of the willow, the air was still. Over by the railings, workmen were holding a shouted conversation, but down here the only sound was the gentle trickle of water from the river, hens clucking somewhere further along and the bees buzzing purposefully around the lavender and rosemary bushes. The door latch moved stiffly. Such a beautiful shed. Surely Fran couldn't really have been serious about taking the front off? I'd fight that tooth and nail if anyone else suggested it. It would be sacrilege.

I pulled open the door with an almost painful sense of expectation. It would serve me right if it was merely a dusty shell.

It wasn't. As soon as I stepped inside, old scents murmured in the air, feeding me dry, papery memories of herb bundles hanging from the rafters. I strained my eyes to accustom my sight to the interior. The shed was so dim where it should have been open to the light that I could almost date its last professional use by the length of time the willows would have taken to spread up this far from the river.

My vision cleared and I caught my breath. Tools were indeed racked along one side of the shed, slightly rusted, but useable. On the opposite side, below the long, cobwebby rectangle of window, was a workbench with wooden seed boxes stacked on top and a tall wooden stool tucked underneath. The stitch in my chest increased. It was as if the resident gardener had simply stepped out for a minute. I could almost see his tin mug of tea and a hunk of bread and cheese on a plate on the end of the bench. I would *kill* to have a shed like this. It was perfect. A whisper of longing crept through me. Never mind the light levels, this was my place and I wanted to work in here so much it hurt. I selected a trowel and a hand fork, the smooth ash handles fitting easily into my palms, and felt the longing turn solid in my stomach.

'I'll use them properly,' I whispered to the shed. 'I promise.'

Outside, I began excavating the lower bed, scraping away at the warm hard-baked soil. I stripped off my early-morning jumper, but otherwise was unaware of the sun's passage overhead, unaware of my hair escaping from my scarf. My phone earpiece pinged gently from time to time with email alerts. They could wait until later. The brick I'd found turned out to be one of a line, running the whole depth of the bed from front to back. Strange. I started to clear to the left of the line and found another narrow brick separator a foot away from the first.

And another one beyond that. There were more on the right of the line, all arranged radially, presumably for decorative purposes, since a single brick's depth wouldn't keep even the most docile roots contained.

Fran came down, shot some footage and left. I sat back on my heels, tendrils of hair clinging sweatily to my face, a mound of vegetation at my side destined for bonfire and compost heap, and looked at what I'd uncovered. It was beautiful and I was entirely flummoxed. I'd never seen anything like it before. Within the broad curving sweep, the bed had been divided up like the spokes of a wheel.

Something about the design tugged at my memory. A passage in an old book. 'They have planted a herb dial down by the river,' I murmured.

'*What* did you say?' A loud voice, shocking in the drowsy silence, made me leap up and spin around, my heart hammering.

A man stood behind me, staring at

me with wild disbelief. He wore a faded short-sleeved shirt and a pair of ancient fawn chinos with traces of earth clinging to the hems. Was he something to do with the TV crew? The rest of them, bar Coralie, had been dressed in what I thought of as designer grunge.

'What did you say?' he repeated.

'Sorry,' I said, my heart rate slowing down again after the shock he'd given me. 'I've been talking for the camera and didn't realise I'd spoken aloud.'

'Yes, but what did you mean?' There was an undercurrent of urgency to his tone.

He was making me nervous. Who was he? 'It was just something I read when I was studying old herb gardens and designs for my degree,' I said awkwardly. 'An account by a medieval traveller, I think. 'They have planted a herb dial down by the river.' I can't remember where it referred to, but the phrase stuck in my memory because it sounded pretty. I've never made a dial bed myself, but I reckon this might be one.'

The man glanced past me at the area I'd cleared. His eyes widened. Then he took a deep breath and seemed to pull himself together. 'It could be, couldn't it? How far down do the bricks go?'

'It's just a single course.'

'Decorative more than practical, then. All these years and I never knew it was here.' He stuck a hand sideways. 'Theo Grainger.'

I shook it. 'Jen Matlock. Wild About Herbs.'

'Ah, right. Bruce told me you were on board. I'm the heritage-vegetable man from next door.' He shot another look at the bed. 'You must be about ready for a break, judging by what you've cleared already. What are you doing for lunch? The Ferry Inn has reasonable bar meals.'

Bar meals meant spending money I didn't have. 'I brought sandwiches with me,' I said, 'but I'd love tea if you know where the kitchen is.' I remembered something else. 'Oh, and I ought to check with Coralie that it was all right to use the tools from the shed. Fran liked them. She said they added authenticity.'

He glanced down at my trowel and hand fork. 'It'll be fine. The whole place has been hired.' His gaze slid towards the shed. 'I had no idea that was there either. It's something else I can't see from my side.'

'The willows and brambles mask an awful lot, don't they?' I said. 'They wouldn't have been in the way when the garden was first laid out, of course. There'd be just the one tree, down by the water's edge. Do you know if your land once belonged to the estate? From the terrace, it looks as though it should all join together and I can't think where else a kitchen garden would go. It would give a more balanced feel to the layout of the grounds as well.'

There was the tiniest of pauses before Theo replied.

'This whole area used to be Wansdale estate land. Death duties are terrible things. I'll take you to the kitchen. I'm told once the catering trucks get here, we're entitled to three meals a day and as much tea as we can drink. Unfortunately, that won't be until they're actually filming, so for now it's the kettle or the pub.'

The kitchen was large and full of people talking television shop. Theo ungallantly left me at the back door, but Coralie called his name, darting over to lay a detaining hand on his arm. Maybe it was my imagination, but it looked to me as if he only stayed reluctantly. Theo Grainger, I concluded, was a loner. The crowd didn't bother me, this talkative, earnest, jargon-ridden bunch was nothing compared to my family when we got together with my uncle and aunt and all the cousins. Still, it was too nice a day to be cooped up inside. As soon as I'd made tea, I escaped to get my sandwiches from the van and take them down to the garden. I felt Theo's eyes follow me. I was a teeny bit sorry for him, but not enough to rescue him.

Sitting in the shady doorway of the

shed, I fished my phone out of my pocket and checked my emails as I ate. I really must ask about the WiFi here before this month's allowance ran out, but just now it was more important to mentally stack up the work waiting for me at home.

That done, I started on a sketch of the herb dial as I might restock it. Looking for something to balance my sketchbook on, I spied a sloping box tucked under the workbench, pretending to be a section of woodwork.

I felt a prickle of interest. The box slotted in there so beautifully it must have been made for the space. Maybe it had been used for keeping accounts, or jotting down gardening notes. That would be fantastic. Even lists of seeds from fifty years ago were gold dust where historical understanding was concerned.

I eased it out. It slid readily to hand and proved to be a proper lap desk, perfect for resting my sketchbook on. The writing slope itself was locked, but gardeners were canny. The key would be somewhere nearby — or it would have been at one time. Hung up in the rafters maybe. I'd look for it later. For now I thanked the unknown gardener for the gift of the slope. I really needed to get my thoughts down about the herb dial.

Through the waving fronds of non-period pampas grass along the edge of the upper beds, I noticed Theo Grainger hurrying down the path from the top of the garden. He saw me, stopped abruptly, and turned away. Perhaps he realised I was working and didn't want to disturb me. That would be quite surprising because his brusqueness earlier hadn't given me the impression of sensitivity. Perhaps he was simply scarred from having had to be polite to everyone in the kitchen. Whatever the reason, I was grateful. I didn't have time to waste in conversation, be it of the gardening variety or about television matters.

Returning to my sketch and making a list of the plants already here and the ones I would need to bring in, I became aware of a tiny sliver of white marring the planed oak side of the writing box.

I looked more closely. A fragment of paper, it seemed to be, sticking out of the join between box and lid. It must have been trapped the last time the lid had been shut. I teased at it gently with a fingernail and the very tip of my knife, willing it to come free, ready to stop if I felt anything tear. As more came slowly into view, I realised it was a page from a small pocketbook or a diary. The edge was flimsy and ragged where it had long ago come away from the binding, the paper very thin, as supple as a leaf from an old prayer book. There was writing on the page, blue-black ink in a neat, even script. The words danced for a moment, then settled.

May 1915: I have a refuge at last. The shed, for now, is all mine. Here I can be me. Here I can write down what I dare not say in the house. This terrible war brings strange consola-tions.

My heart thumped. 1915. The box was over a hundred years old. Had I stumbled on a secret from the very era in which the documentary was being filmed?

3

May 1915: I have a refuge at last . . .

I sat in the shade of the willows, staring at the writing, shaken by this voice from the past coming so aptly on what Coralie had rattled off this morning regarding the script for the documentary. It was a very large assumption with nothing except gut feeling to go on — and it would be extraordinary if it was true — but the word *refuge*, taken with the date and the letter from Lady Mary mentioning Louise being difficult, suggested this was a page from that very same Louise's diary. The fact that it had been locked in a hidden box reinforced the idea. I was jumping to conclusions, but the date was bang on, and who else from the house would have access to the shed? I wondered what it was that she couldn't say aloud. Something about the war? Something about the soldiers? Something about herself? I stared at the page some more. Should I tell Coralie about it? She might want to add it to the manor memorabilia. And yet . . . and yet . . .

And yet I didn't want this flimsy page all jumbled up with the other ephemera in those trays. The page belonged in the writing desk and the desk belonged here in the shed. It had been hidden for a purpose. If this was Louise's diary, she might have sat right where I was, writing it. Did aristocratic young ladies sit on potting shed steps back then? No, that was daft. If she needed a refuge that badly, she'd have written her diary *inside* the shed. There would have been plenty of light coming through the window a hundred years ago. The rest of the diary would tell me, if I could only get at it. I twisted to look up at the rafters and along the length of the bench, trying to figure out if there was anywhere that the key to the writing slope might be hidden. Hopeless. It was far too dim without a torch and in all likelihood the key was long since lost anyway. Besides, there was no time to look for it. I had a job to do or I wouldn't get paid. A possible secret from a hundred years ago could wait. I continued roughing out my plan of the herb dial. Out of the corner of my eye, I noticed a small group of people at the top of the garden. A rake-thin man, who radiated such concentrated power that he had to be Bruce the director, was being filmed talking to Coralie. Theo, heading around the side from the fantastical stable, hesitated for a split second, drew back, then at Bruce's imperious gesture, joined them. They started down the steps towards me. Without conscious thought, I pushed the writing slope back into its concealed space under the bench. The loose diary page I slipped between a fold of kitchen paper in my sandwich box before snapping the lid shut.

I didn't stop to ask myself why I was hiding my finds. It was done purely on instinct. I think I already felt the shed was mine. Its secrets — whatever they were — were my secrets. I had taken on a duty to protect them as soon as I'd fitted the gardener's trowel to my palm. There was also the rather muddled thought that after a century when those words could have been discovered by anyone, anyone at all, they had waited and come to me. I needed space to absorb that. I had learned the hard way about the consequences of hasty actions. I wasn't going to rush this. The diary page could simmer in the back of my mind while I got on with more urgent tasks.

I ran my hand along the tools, lifted a border fork from the rack and crossed to the herb dial to resume work, feeling the ghosts of past nurserymen padding alongside me. I chuckled. Even without the willows and the pampas grass, the shed's concealed position relative to the house must have been advantageous to whole generations of gardeners sneaking a quick break whilst still watching out for their employers. I wouldn't put it past them to have carefully sited it here for that very reason.

The group of people grew nearer. The man with Coralie was indeed Bruce and, as it turned out, his destination was me. In a set of lightning decisions, he approved the dial bed, dismissed the shed except as background and told Coralie to sort out a scaffold for a fixed camera. 'Your suggestion of putting the herbs on your side wouldn't have been accurate at all,' he said in a dismissive fashion to Theo. 'This is better.' Bruce's eyes glinted with fanaticism as he gazed around. 'This is *right*. I feel it. We can have Louise down here picking herbs with the wounded soldiers on the terrace behind her.' And then to me, almost in the same breath, 'Tell me about the design. What do the spokes signify?'

Fran's camera swooped across to me. Pushing away the collywobbles in my stomach, I gripped the handle of the fork for courage. The smooth honest wood bolstered me. 'They're just decorative, I think. They complement the shape of the beds. The divisions would have been useful to eliminate mistakes when directing apprentices or garden boys as to what to gather. For instance, if thyme was planted in the third radial along from the right, the head gardener could describe the position of the herb he wanted his assistant to pick, but he wouldn't need to be on the spot himself overseeing the work.'

'So, not symbolic, then?' I couldn't tell from Bruce's inflexion whether he was disappointed or merely clearing possibilities out of the way.

'Maybe,' I said. 'I know I've read something somewhere about a herb dial, but I don't remember the shape being mentioned as significant. I doubt it had any particular meaning. Gardeners generally tend towards the practical rather than the mystical.'

There was a suppressed snort of laughter, but I didn't dare look to see who had made it. My money was on Theo.

Bruce brooded for a moment, his

eyes on the bed. 'Look up that reference,' he said at last. And then they were gone, hurrying up the garden as purposefully as they had descended.

Theo lingered. 'Why thyme?' he asked. 'All the plants you could have mentioned. Why pick on thyme?'

I shrugged. 'It was just an example. Thyme is one of the most ubiquitous herbs you find in old kitchen gardens.' I eyed him curiously. 'Does it matter? Are you interested for a reason?'

He turned on his heel. 'Not particularly.'

And that was a fib if ever I'd heard one. Still, it was none of my business. I set my foot on the shoulder of the fork, pushing the tines firmly into the gritty soil of the herb dial. There was a lot to dig before I could start planting. I threw a silent promise to Louise — if it *was* Louise — that I wouldn't forget to look for the key to the writing desk. I also promised her I wouldn't do anything hasty if I discovered what she had written. The same sun that warmed my back now had warmed hers a hundred years ago. Her hands had gripped the handle of a border fork, just as mine were doing. We had a bond.

For now, though, I needed to put my back into the paid job. I emptied my mind and simply got on with it. I didn't think about the filming, my business, my family, secret diaries, anything. There was pleasure in this, breaking the clods down, sifting out old roots, seeing the earth raked fresh, ready for new planting. I ended up not having a break at all, with the result that by the time I finished for the day, it was far too dim inside the shed to search for anything. I went up to the house, wondering if I ought to sign out in some fashion, and was surprised to find technicians still laying cables and Coralie making coffee for herself and Bruce in the kitchen.

'Still at it?' I asked, somewhat unnecessarily.

'We start early and work late on a shoot, especially when we've only just got in,' she explained, rubbing the back of her neck. 'The scaffold tower is arriving first thing tomorrow, by the way. Bruce wants a time-lapse sequence of the herb dial progress for the 'making-of' film.'

'A film about a film? How on earth do you keep straight what's happening when?'

She smiled briefly. 'It's just part of the project. Some productions use a separate EPK team, but Bruce likes to keep everything in house.' Her hand went to her nape again.

My eyes followed the movement with a fatalistic resignation. I was hungry, my back ached, I wanted a shower, and I had several hours of Wild About Herbs work waiting at home. But I was a doctor's daughter and, as Chris was a bit too fond of saying, I never have been able to hold off when someone seems to me to be in trouble. He generally added the rider 'whether they want you to or not'.

I put my satchel down. 'Would you like me to massage your neck before I go? I know what I'm doing. I always sort out Dad's back when I'm at home and he's a GP.'

Coralie looked Britishly scandalised at the very thought of accepting a chance-met massage from someone without a couch, white coat and full set of certificates.

'No, I'll be fine,' she said. 'I've got painkillers. I'll book an appointment with my surgery when we've finished the shoot. Thanks anyway.'

I hesitated, but I couldn't just walk away. 'Painkillers only mask the problem,' I said. 'Massage can start the repair. At the very least it'll relax the affected muscles and make it less likely that you exacerbate any inflammation by tensing up. I promise it will help. If what I do is in the least bit uncomfortable, just tell me to stop.'

Coralie's hands twisted together indecisively. 'I suppose there *is* that scene in the script where Louise does massage,' she said. 'Several of the soldiers wrote letters mentioning that they felt more mobile after she'd rubbed in some sort of lavender cream. We could count this as research.' She brightened up, talking herself into it. 'And then, if you're competent at it, we could use *you* rather than get a professional on board. That would be much better for continuity. Bruce would like that.' She dropped into a chair. 'Go on, then.'

I shook my head in mystification. Media people were so weird. She wouldn't take help for herself, but she would for the sake of the television programme? Talk about dedicated. I moved her hair and rested my fingers lightly against her skin in assessment. I wasn't expecting the shock that ran through me. Coralie was so tense she could snap any second. No wonder her neck ached. Dad would have prescribed a cat to stroke in an instant. And yet she projected such an air of control. It just showed you could never go by appearances. I breathed out, balancing myself. This was why I preferred plants to people. They were far less complicated.

From my pack, I added a drop of lavender massage oil to my fingertips. Lavender for relaxation. If anyone needed to relax, it was this woman. I braced myself, started slowly and closed my eyes as I worked, telling her to drop her chin, pushing gently into the muscles either side of her spine, making long movements, feeling where the problem was.

'This is nice,' said Coralie in a surprised voice after a moment. 'It hurts, but in a good way, if you know what I mean. I can feel everything easing. Did you never think of taking it up?'

I paused before I spoke, arranging my words with care. 'I'm a bona fide first-aider, but the qualifications for professional physiotherapy take quite a while and a terrible lot of book work. I wasn't comfortable enough with that to spend so much time away from making a living.'

'Oh, right,' she said, as if this made

perfect sense. I felt a little guilty at misleading her, but it was better than admitting the truth.

The thing was, this sort of limited healing was so much a part of me that until I was twelve I hadn't realised everyone didn't have the same innate ability. Then my cousin Kevin got into an unfair fight in the playground. I saw red and charged into the melee to stop it. The older boy hitting him was furious at the ignominy of a girl interfering and pushed me out of the way to wrench at Kevin's arm. Kevin screamed in pain, the other boy faltered and I instinctively barged him aside to take hold of Kevin's shoulder and fix it.

Afterwards, I was told repeatedly and at length that his shoulder had been dislocated and I could have done untold harm by moving it. At the time I had no knowledge of dislocation, but as soon as I touched Kevin the wrongness was so raw and strong that I could see exactly how to pull his shoulder and ease it back into place to relieve the pain. It was like a living diagram burnt into my brain. I could no more have not done it than I could have flown.

He was tearfully grateful. 'Oh, Jen, thank you. That was horrible.'

I shrugged, feeling bruises form across my back where the other boy had repeatedly thumped me while I was shielding Kevin. 'That's okay.'

Kevin got a warning for fighting and was sent home for the rest of the day to recover. The other boy was suspended. I got detention.

'But I wasn't fighting,' I said indignantly. 'I *stopped* the fight. I was fixing Kevin's shoulder.'

'Stupid girl. You could have made it ten times worse. You should have left him where he was until the ambulance arrived,' replied the PE teacher.

'What ambulance?' I said, aggrieved. 'The teachers hadn't even seen there was a fight. Kevin was *hurting*.'

And that, as Dad said later when I was raging about the unfairness of the teachers being cross and yelling about not meddling with things I knew nothing about, and not even listening when I told them I'd been able to feel what was wrong, had probably contributed to the punishment. No one in authority likes it pointed out to them by a twelve-year-old that they aren't doing their job properly.

I muttered that they hadn't listened to Kevin either when he told them he'd been in agony and I'd made it better. Coincidence, they had said shortly, and added I should thank my lucky stars that I'd got away with it.

And now I was late home and starving and Mum, being a teacher herself, had been just a little bit inclined to side with the school.

Dad passed me the packet of hobnobs he kept in his drawer. 'What you need,' he said thoughtfully, 'is the St John's Ambulance First Aid course.'

I'd looked at him, watery-eyed.

'I know you could feel what was wrong,' he said. 'Just between you and me, it runs in the family. I had a feeling it had come down to you. But people are strange and it'll do you no harm to learn the technical terms. It's about time you did. Certificates, Jen, are remarkably useful things. As are nice visible pin badges should something like this happen again.'

'I'm still cross,' I said, but it wasn't so bad, knowing he understood.

He ruffled my hair. 'I don't blame you. Go and dig the vegetable patch until teatime. Get it out of your system.'

I did a lot of digging of that vegetable patch over the years, and if I was still cross when I'd finished ours, I'd take the bus to Granny's house and dig hers. When you have three older brothers all telling you to 'Go and play, Jen,' instead of letting you join in with the far more interesting things they are doing, you tend to need something to take your feelings out on. Mind you, they were all quite happy for me to look after them when they'd fallen off bikes and given themselves a black eye (Ewan), been beaten up by bullies at school for being clever (Anthony), or tumbled out of trees and off walls (Chris, constantly). Over the years I'd bathed cuts and grazes, strapped up sprains, splinted breaks, anointed bruises and tied slings. I'm not sure any of them realised what I was actually doing. They just thought it was a girl-thing. Or maybe they did realise and felt guilty about me being uncomplainingly there whenever they needed me. Perhaps that was why they were so protective of me the whole time. Because I was different.

* * *

None of this, naturally, did I mention to Coralie right now. I just let it hurry through my mind. I didn't spend too long on her neck this first session, but I did leave her more relaxed. I said I'd repeat the massage if she was still tense tomorrow. Having had little to no sleep last night, I was reeling with tiredness by now, and it was becoming critical that I have something to eat and a sit down. Heading for my van and hoping I'd replaced the emergency bar of chocolate I'd eaten last week after that guy had cracked a rib at the re-enactment fair, I was surprised to see Theo spreading gravel on the drive. He had his phone on loudspeaker as he shovelled, apologising to a customer for having omitted to pack her a list of the veg box contents this week. I smiled as he identified her querulous description of 'round green Martian globes with little bits of leaf sprouting out of the top' as kohlrabi. 'Peel and slice,' he said cheerfully. 'It adds a lovely crunch to a salad.'

'I didn't know kohlrabi was an old vegetable,' I said when he'd finished the call.

'I grow standard varieties alongside the heritage ones — have to or I wouldn't make a living — but as it happens there are references for kohlrabi going back to Roman times. Are you okay? You look all in.'

Oh thanks. Just what a girl wants to hear when she's trying to project herself as calmly efficient. 'Just hungry,' I said, and nodded at the mound of gravel. 'Why is this you?'

He shrugged. 'I didn't see anyone else spreading it.'

If that was a hint, I didn't take it. I was massively tired and still had online orders to fill when I got home. All the same, it was odd.

4

I got home to see that the developers had succeeding in chasing another of my neighbours off the site. When St Martin's Primary had closed, part of the deal had been that the school would be let in discrete units to small start-up businesses at affordable rates. I rented the caretaker's cottage, miniature sports hall, toolshed and playing field for Wild About Herbs. An artisan bakery rented the school kitchens and two classrooms. A printing firm, gifts & promotions company and an art studio parcelled up the rest between them.

Which was all lovely, except the council changed their mind three years down the line and decided what the neighbourhood really needed was a supermarket. The developers who had persuaded them of this turned out to be the sort who viewed notice periods as the time you could spend making life increasingly unpleasant for the sitting tenants.

I waved a sad goodbye to Kelly from the St Martin's Bakery and promised I'd deliver her next herb order to her new premises as soon as she was up and running. In return I got a bag of misshapen rolls of varying flavours for my freezer. This, together with the care package Mum had pressed on me as we'd left yesterday, sorted out my immediate meal needs nicely.

As I ate and started on the evening's work, I thought about what I'd told Coralie earlier. What I did wasn't so much healing as kick-starting the body into healing for itself. Unlike Dad, I'd never had any desire to be a GP. Most of his work seemed to be talking to patients and filling in forms, rather than hands-on action. I'd wanted something dashing and physical. Something *not* cerebral and bristling with accolades like my super-intelligent brothers were working towards. Sports physio, perhaps? I could fancy that. I'd be out there on the Olympics track or behind the scenes in a Premier league locker room. That would do. The thought that maybe, just possibly, Mum might one day find something to boast about regarding *me* in the Christmas round-robin never crossed my mind. Not once. Ahem.

But . . . learning bored me unless it was something I was interested in. Maybe I'd just get a job as a Premier League groundsman instead. Looking after lawns took no effort at all.

'No, Jen, you've *got* to go to university,' Chris told me the first vacation after he'd gone up to Cambridge. 'You really must. It's fantastic.'

He did seem amazingly happy, and by then — with just me left behind at home — I was desperate to get away from the full force of Mum's attention and the disappointed gaze whenever she saw me weeding rather than doing my homework. So I pulled up my academic socks and applied myself. I scraped into my insurance choice university reading sports physiotherapy and, as Chris had promised, thoroughly enjoyed my first month of independence. Right up until the moment when an event I was first-aiding at needed my skills.

I should explain that Dad has this thing about everyone having a duty to use the talents they've been given. The St John's Ambulance are also pretty clear that if you benefit from their training, you repay by volunteering at public events. I'd done it ever since I'd got that first junior certificate and now, seeing my university had a live action role-playing club, I volunteered to turn up as a first-aider at their weekend sessions. My friends might stare at this waste of free time, but it suited me. I had no wish to dress up and role-play myself. I did enjoy being of practical use. Why jog or do aerobics to get fit when you could dig and weed instead? Why lie on the bed and read when you could bring your book to an event like this and patch people up between chapters?

There was a lot of patching up. Right from the word go it was borne in on me that LARPers had the least sense of self-preservation of any group of people I'd ever met. Once they were in character, they never even saw the trees they ran into or the rabbit holes they turned ankles in. It was astonishing what damage they could cheerfully wreak on themselves when running through mud in cloaks and medieval costumes, skirmishing with beautifully created solid latex weapons. True, it was mostly light stuff: strained tendons, nettle rashes and the sort of hand injuries that follow over-enthusiastic instances of pole-arm fighting, for instance. It could still cause serious inconvenience the following Monday in lectures if not treated. On the particular occasion when my lovely new life had started to unravel, a marsh-dweller who had been a bit too literal in her interpretation of webbed toes got her foot trampled by sixteen stone of ooze monster. As I cleaned her foot, I suggested that even web-footed marsh dwellers with convincingly slimy leggings should probably wear boots when engaging in hand-to-hand combat in the woods.

She nodded, white faced with pain. 'I will next time. Is it broken?'

At this, the ooze monster who had carried her across to me repeating 'Sorry, sorry, I'm so sorry' the whole time, looked even greener than she did in her face-paint.

I finished swabbing her foot clean and laid hands on it, conscientiously applying what I'd been learning since term began, and found . . . nothing. I tried again. Really nothing. To my complete and absolute horror, I couldn't sense the bones or ligaments or anything beyond her puffy, discoloured skin. I had to frantically empty my mind before I could even dimly feel what was wrong. 'Just bruised and strained,' I said, hoping she couldn't hear the shake in my voice. I applied a cold compress and told her to take painkillers and arnica tablets for the next couple of days. Just what any first-aider would have done. But I wasn't any first-aider. I was better than that. Much better. Where had it all gone?

The incident shook me horribly. I don't think I slept at all that night, going over and over the ghastliness of that empty, barren moment in my mind. It was as if thinking by the book about what I was doing interfered with my ability to work intuitively. The top part of my brain was so busy analysing possible scenarios that the subconscious didn't have space to *feel*. The prospect of losing a gift that was so much a part of me was terrifying. It was a nightmare. What could I do?

At some base level, I knew that if I stopped studying, the gift would come back. I wanted it back. I couldn't face life without it. It was part of me. On the other hand, as Chris had prophesied, I loved university. I loved the freedom, the liberation of making my own decisions. I loved dressing for me, not for family or school. I loved eating what

I liked, when I liked. I didn't want to chuck it all and go home. It would look like defeat.

Feeling thoroughly miserable, I'd stared out of my student bedroom window as dawn spread a delicate rosy wash over the horticulture fields in the distance. There had to be a solution. Had to be. As things stood, I had a choice. I could carry on with the degree and hope that one day I'd be able to meld my gift with the book-learning, the same way I did with first aid. Or I could finish university right now, unlearn everything, get a boring job and rent a bedsit (I was so not going home again) simply to be able to use my talent as it had been given to me.

I paced the room, wishing, for the first time since Dad dropped me off at the beginning of term, that I was back at home where I could dig over the flower bed to help me think.

Oh.

Flower beds.

A wave of relief broke over me. There

was a third alternative after all.

I could switch to a horticulture degree. Plants. Herbs. Digging, Growing. Something outdoor-based and useful. I even had the right A-levels because botany was a subject that had always interested me as being useful and practical. It would mean I could stay here, consolidate my freedom, get a degree and heal my bruised talent.

I didn't tell them at home until the switch was a done deal. Mum was deeply disappointed. A degree in gardening wouldn't carry anything like the same panache as becoming a sports physio. I told her the course had been too academic for me, something she accepted with unflattering alacrity. Dad understood though, tactfully forbearing to comment on my taking up a subject awash with Latin names. Mum did come around marginally when I did a year at Kew later on and got my part-time master's in historical gardening. I still think the thing she was most impressed by was when I mentioned I'd been Alan Titchmarsh's minder the day he came to give a guest lecture.

In general though, I was still Jen-the-girl, Jen-the-youngest, Jen-the-last-but-by-no-means-least. Really, I wouldn't be surprised if she privately called me Jen Herbs herself.

My earpiece pinged softly, reminding me of the real world. Enough introspection. I needed to get on with tonight's work. The orders weren't going to fill themselves.

5

I was not best pleased, when I arrived at Wansdale Manor next morning, to find Theo Grainger in the garden, hunkered down in front of the herb dial and squinting diagonally between the willows towards his barn on the other side of the boundary railings. I'd go so far as to say I regarded the crouched figure with considerable bitterness. I'd got here early so I could search for the key to the writing desk before anyone else was about. I'd had too little sleep for the second night in a row and if I'd known Theo was going to be my side of the railings at this god-forsaken hour I'd have grabbed another twenty minutes in bed.

'You're here in good time,' he said, straightening up as I came down the path. Interestingly, his expression smoothed from put out to politely inquiring in exactly the same way mine was doing.

'I need to finish the digging,' I said, possibly not in the friendliest tone in the world. 'I have to get the plants in as soon as possible if I'm to make this bed look established. What brings you to my part of the garden?'

'Mystery leak in the barn roof. I wondered if I might be able to see a hole from this side.'

'And can you?' He must have phenomenal vision if so.

'No,' he said. 'Back to Plan A.'

'Which is?'

'Put buckets down. See you later.' He nodded at me and ambled up towards the house.

I watched him go with narrowed eyes. Leak indeed. We hadn't had a decent rainstorm in weeks. What was he up to? A lifetime of staying one step ahead of three older brothers was telling me very strongly that some misdirection was being practised here. To my further exasperation, I'd only just opened the shed when loud voices and a clanging of poles heralded the arrival of the scaffolders.

'Jen, don't do anything more to the bed for the moment,' called Coralie, hurrying down the path. 'This won't take long. Once the camera's fixed, we can start the time-lapse sequence. My neck feels marvellous, by the way.'

She was in designer flatties today, I noticed. Nothing if not adaptable, our Coralie. She evidently accessorised herself to match the terrain. 'You still need to go to the doctor to get a referral to a proper physiotherapist,' I warned her. 'They'll give you exercises to stop you tensing up. Also advice on posture so the problem doesn't come back.'

'Yes, yes,' she said, with the assurance of one who knows her deportment has been faultless since the day she was born. She glanced at her computer tablet. 'Now then, did you find that herb dial reference for Bruce?'

I gaped at her. 'No, I, er . . . ' For goodness' sake, he'd only mentioned it yesterday afternoon. When was I supposed to have gone through my books?

'Try the research room. It might be in some of the stuff we've accumulated there.'

I very much doubted it, as I had a memory of having found it in a reference work on something else entirely, but I might as well take a look. I wouldn't be able to do anything on the herb dial until the scaffolders had finished. I shut the shed door crossly. I should definitely have had that extra sleep.

As I was in the house, I made a mug of tea in the kitchen. Biscuits, bread and a toaster had now been added to the tea, coffee and kettle on the worktop. Coralie making sure everyone kept up their energy levels, presumably. One end of the cavernous room was being transformed into an Edwardian filming area under the direction of a motherly-looking woman with a no-nonsense northern accent who knew exactly what she wanted where. She certainly wasn't having any truck with the set designer who was viewing the assorted vintage kitchen equipment with an artistic, rather than practical eye. I backed away and left them to it.

In complete contrast, sun streamed through the French windows of the quiet terrace room, laying dancing dust stripes across the bookcases and trays of letters and photographs. It really was a gem of a room. If I lived in the manor, I didn't think I'd ever move out of it.

What with tea and the calm and permission to have a legitimate rummage through the gardening almanacs, I began to feel human again. I sat on the floor to investigate the lower shelves where the older volumes were. Bliss. A few minutes later, a soft sound alerted me to the fact that there was someone at a table at the far end, skimming through glossy coffee-table books. I craned my neck to look.

'Theo!' I said in astonishment. What was he doing here? Did the man not have any of his own work to do? First he turned up in my herb patch, now he was in the research room. I'd dearly love to know the secret of taking so much time off while still running a full-time, hands-on business.

'I thought there might be photos of the walled garden as it used to be,' he said, though I hadn't asked what he was doing. 'It could be useful for the programme to know what it looked like in the days before the place was split and my side was turned into a business.'

Okay, maybe I'd misjudged him. 'When your part of the grounds was the kitchen garden for the manor, you mean? Yes, it would be interesting, but you couldn't change the layout now, could you? Not just for the filming. Not when your crops are already growing and you've got customers waiting.'

The tiny hint slid past him. 'No, but it would be something to mention on camera when they are expecting me to say a few erudite words. You've surely noticed how keen Bruce is for everything to be as authentic as possible.

Besides . . . ' He hesitated. ' . . . don't laugh, but I sometimes find myself knowing that potatoes, for instance, would do well in a particular place, or brassicas are useless somewhere else. I just wonder whether it's me being fanciful or whether there's a land memory attached to the garden. It would be nice to find out if I was right.'

A land memory? What a wonderful theory. Perhaps he *wasn't* just an idle hobby-gardener. Maybe he did have a proper feeling for the soil. 'Something more than gardener's instinct, you mean? I've come across that sort of vibe in gardens no end of times. There could be photos of the manor gardens, I suppose. I've found herb garden illustrations in old-time guidebooks before now. My gripe is usually that the photographers focused on the general prettiness of the image from afar, rather than taking useful close-ups to help me identify individual plants.'

'Tell me about it,' he said with feeling.

I sipped my tea, eyeing him thoughtfully. If Theo was interested in his side of the garden's history, it might be a way for me to find out about whoever had used my shed in the past without letting Bruce or Coralie know I was holding out on them about the diary page. So, 'Do you know much about the history of the house?' I said, as if I was simply making conversation. 'It's been such a rush since I answered the advert that I haven't had time to look it up myself. I noticed a letter in one of these trays from a Lady Wansdale, so presumably the manor was a family home at the time when this programme is set?'

'Oh yes, the family were here for generations,' he said.

I looked enquiring.

He gave a shrug and crossed to the terrace windows, still carrying the book he'd been leafing through. 'It's been leased out as long as I've been next door, but Wansdale itself goes right back to medieval times. At one point it was ceded to the local abbey, presumably so the Lord

Wansdale of the day would have an assured prayer-assisted passage through to the afterlife when his time came. Then the abbey was dissolved and the Wansdale family, who weren't stupid when it came to reversion clauses, grabbed the estate back.'

An abbey . . . an abbey? Memory hit me. 'Oh! That's it!' I said, scrambling up. 'That's where I saw the herb dial reference.' I reached into my satchel for my phone, then remembered I'd forgotten to charge it last night. Still, there was a laptop on the table nearest me. 'Is there WiFi here? I need to google Reverend Septimus Thomson's *History of Various Monastic Gardens.* '

Theo looked at me with the sort of bemused-but-willing-to-be-entertained expression familiar to me from my brothers and cousins. 'Who?' he said.

I grinned. 'Isn't it a glorious name? He was a Victorian parson who collected odds and ends of information about old religious establishments and put all the extracts higgledy-piggledy into a book. I'm sure that was where I found the passage.'

'Which passage?'

I powered up the laptop. Theo strolled over and watched over my shoulder as I searched. 'The herb dial one. There, that's it,' I said, clicking on the right reference. 'I remember now. I've never seen a real copy, but this was part of a project to scan neglected texts on to the internet. I found Rev Septimus's ramblings when I was doing my dissertation on historic design.' I scrolled rapidly through the pages. 'There it is,' I said triumphantly. 'I knew I hadn't imagined it.' My voice rose in excitement as I read on. 'Theo! It's *here* he was talking about! Listen to this. In 1229, a traveller by the name of John Goode was lodged at Wansdale Manor by the monks of the local abbey and described the setting: *They have built a herb dial down by the river for the better easement of all manner of ailments. The situation is sweet and the Brothers diligent. Produce is plentiful* due to its peculiar climate and unusual warmth. The monks' honey is accounted most superior and mends all manner of bodily injuries as well as being the finest I ever tasted. There is a rhyme attached to the property, which goes thus:

> Wansdale land holds Wansdale bounty
> Richest — '

The book Theo was holding fell out of his grasp on to the keyboard. By some freak of chance, the corner of it hit the power button. The screen instantly blacked out.

'Sorry,' said Theo. 'Still, at least you can tell Bruce it was a herb dial now, though whether it would still have been used in that form during 1915 won't be known unless we find a photograph. Talking of which, have you seen the photos of when the house was a convalescent hospital during WW1? There's a whole collection of them. The local paper had them in their archives. MovingInk are going to mock up a ward in the dining room. Coralie says they've sourced some original tubular-framed beds for the patients. Can you believe it? You'd think they'd have rusted away by now. It might be easiest if you parked your van inside the stable block once the props trucks roll in.'

It was the most verbose I'd heard him yet. I was so surprised at the sudden unprovoked flow of information that I allowed him to steer me over to the table where the ephemera baskets were. Yes, it was a transparent distraction to get me away from the internet, but I'd figure out why he was doing it later. I had seen what I wanted to see.

I listened with interest as Theo told me about the Wansdale men who had gone to war and not come back, thus heralding crippling death duties and the start of the manor's decline. Inside I was speculating. He'd dropped the book deliberately, I was sure. What he didn't know was that he'd been too late. My eyes had already scanned ahead to the rest of the rhyme.

Wansdale land holds Wansdale bounty
Richest prize in all the county
Thyme on dial leads arrow straight
Through the wall and o'er the gate

And he'd mentioned thyme yesterday and he'd been down at the herb dial checking out lines of sight early this morning. Was there something the tiniest bit shady about our heritage-veg man from next door? I added up two plus two, plus another two again. *Richest prize in all the county.* Maybe I was jumping to conclusions, but the answer kept coming out as treasure hunting.

I leafed though the basket as Theo talked. Underneath a grainy clutch of stiff, posed hospital photos was the 1914 letter I had noticed yesterday from Lady Mary Wansdale. There was another with it, dated 1915, also addressed to 'My dear Evelyn'. Presumable this Evelyn had kept all her correspondence, as ladies often did in those days. Her descendants must have disposed of it and Bruce's researchers had bought it. I didn't hold out any great hopes that Lady Mary had itemised all the garden plants to her friend, but you never knew. I read the letter anyway, especially when I saw it was about Louise.

Louise has joined the VAD Red Cross nurses. You will be surprised at my change of heart, my dear Evelyn, after I was so against the idea when she raised the subject of applying to the Queen Alexandra regiment, but I have my reasons and I think you will approve of them once you know all!

First, we have been informed that this house is to be requisitioned as an auxiliary convalescent hospital for our brave troops. (We can, naturally, stay in our own wing.) Second, I have made it clear that Louise is only to be stationed here, and will not be permitted to go abroad. That would serve no purpose at all.

Third — and, I make no bones

about this, my dear Evelyn, as we have often discussed it between ourselves — there is no denying that Louise is a plain girl. The injured officers, however, will be gentlemen! Not eldest sons, I don't suppose, even though dear Freddy thought it his duty to go. That would be too much to hope for, but I daresay some may have small estates. It is established fact that a gentleman injured in his country's service is very likely to become much attached to a good, sweet girl in a nurse's cap who alleviates his pain or distracts him by reading to him when the discomfort is very bad. Louise has quite pretty ankles, which they are bound to notice and which is the only agreeable circumstance regarding shorter-length dresses.

Sadly, I doubt that there will be a rich, injured officer amongst the convalescents, but a respectable marriage will do. And if all that fails, it will be in every way proper for her to say that she did her duty to her country when *the Drawing Room presentations begin again after the war is over.*

I read the letter with disbelief. Lady Mary was a monster. I said as much to Coralie when she hurried into the room looking for me.

Theo melted away via the French windows, saying research was all very well, but some people had work to do. I gazed after him indignantly.

'Oh there you are, Jen. Bruce wants to . . . who is a monster? What's that you've got?' asked Coralie. She skimmed the letter. 'No, no, Lady Mary is only doing the best for her daughter. She is going to make the most marvellous character.'

'In that case, she ought to want what makes Louise happy,' I said. 'She should have let her join the Queen Alexandra nurses the previous year, if that's what her daughter wanted. I'd hate to be match-maked like that.'

'That is Bruce's point,' said Coralie earnestly. 'Don't you see? It's about the change in attitudes now from how they were then. In those days, parents did decide what would make you happy. Arranged marriages. Not moving out of your own class. The Great War altered things.'

I was more than ever convinced Louise was the writer of my diary page. It was clear she had issues with her mother. If anyone had needed a refuge, it was the daughter of Lady Mary. 'Making *me* happy means leaving me alone,' I said. 'I'd never have survived being Lady Mary's daughter. What about you? What would make you happy?'

Coralie looked slightly wistfully at the letter. 'Well, that really. A nice marriage. A husband who thinks I'm wonderful.'

I made a sceptical face. 'You'd still need something to keep you occupied. Is it okay if I copy these letters?'

'Sure,' she said, indicating a photo-copier in the corner of the room. 'There are some more in the basket. Copy what you like. That's really what started off Bruce's interest. I found all these letters in a country house sale and thought they might be his sort of thing. He got the whole idea of the documentary just reading through them the first time. It was so inspiring to witness, you wouldn't believe. We found a link to the photos on a WW1 memorabilia site, scoured soldiers' letters home and then, when he discovered Wansdale itself might actually be available for filming, Bruce went and camped in his backers' front rooms, explaining the concept over and over until they saw the beauty of the project too.'

I copied the letter as she talked, which was just as well since Bruce himself whirlwinded in (directing a look of crushing disappointment at Coralie, presumably for not instantly transporting me to his side) and whisked me off to talk — completely unprepared — about herb garden design.

It went terribly. I was stiff, my notes were in my satchel, my rough design also. And I hadn't drunk nearly enough tea so far today. When it was over I filled my thermos mug quickly and fled like a homing pigeon for the garden.

The scaffolders were finished. Fran was fixing up the static camera. I sat in the doorway of the shed and began a brand new drawing of the herb dial. I didn't want my faltering effort just now anywhere near a camera lens again.

* * *

'That was a disaster,' announced Bruce matter-of-factly half an hour later as he swept briskly down the garden with a small crew. 'Too stiff and stilted.' He inhaled a great breath of outdoors and spread his arms. '*This* is your milieu, this is your place. I love you on those steps. Stay right there and tell me about herb garden design again.'

'Light levels,' said Fran in a laconic voice.

Bruce's nostrils flared. He swept the terrain like a general and extended a forefinger. 'Bucket,' he said. 'Upend it on the path. No, wait, next to those blue bushes.' He clicked his fingers for me to supply the name.

'Lavender, two different kinds,' I said dutifully.

He nodded, absorbing the information and filing it away. 'Next to the lavender. Sit on the bucket just as you are, no fiddling with your scarf. Untidy is artisan. Wait! Take your earpiece out. Good. Fran, focus on the drawing.'

I'll give him this. He was dead right about it being my place out here. I felt much more relaxed than I had earlier. I took a deep breath of warm lavender air and began again. 'Traditionally, a medieval herb bed had sixteen plants in a square design . . . '

This went better. I could feel it. Bruce confirmed it afterwards. 'It'll need post-production tweaking, but it's useable.' He nodded at my lap. 'I like your drawing slope. It suits you. Suits the image. Authentic. It'll fix you in the minds of the viewers. Keep it in when we do something else you need to illustrate.'

He was gone before I could say anything. I looked down, my stomach plunging horribly. In the rush, I'd forgotten to hide the secret writing desk. And now everyone thought it was mine.

6

I was finally on my own, but I couldn't search for the key to the writing desk, not with the time-lapse camera poised above the herb dial ready to record the transformation. I needed to get on. I slid the desk back, replaced my earpiece and dug my fork into the earth, more than willing to do just that. Quite apart from it being what I was paid for, digging had always calmed me. Turning over the soil and clearing out the last of the old bedding existed on a purely physical level, something my hands and feet and fingers could do while I thought about planting. I could feel myself becoming more balanced by the moment. This was better. This was *me*. The rhythmic pattern of movement was beautifully soothing after the flurry of the morning so far. If I concentrated on the earth, I could almost ignore the camera.

I *hated* being filmed, having to change what I was doing at a moment's notice. How did Coralie look so in control the whole time? She must thrive on nervous energy. As for being constantly alert to the least signal from Bruce . . . well, no wonder she was tense. Ugh, the very thought made my skin crawl. A life in the media wouldn't suit me at all.

It was starting to get warm. I retreated into the shed to change into shorts and apply suncream before I began laying out plants. Having the sort of skin that turns crisp in sunshine was a definite disadvantage in my job. Outside again, I considered the bed. Creating an established garden for the documentary was very different to my usual commission of building some-thing that would start small (and cheap) and attain full growth within a few years. To look convincing, it would need a variety of sizes, as if the bed had been worked over time. Crowding in lots of small plants wouldn't give the right impression. I'd dug up some of my well-grown bushes early this morning and put them in the van, wrapped in damp sacking. Setting these out first would give me an idea of how the herb dial was going to look, then I could adjust my ideas as necessary and bring in the rest of the plants over the course of the week. If nothing else, it would lessen the number of plants I'd have to rehouse once I was evicted. Despite my airy assurances to the family, I wasn't dealing very well with the nursery situation. There was a cold core of panic stopping me making sensible plans, stopping me making any plans at all really. The council had offered me an unused allotment for temporary storage by way of appeasement, but said I couldn't carry on a business from there. I had been to see the allotment. The weeds were edge to edge, chest high and riddled with rusty chain-link fencing. If they thought I was going to reclaim that land at no expense to them, they could think again.

I pushed the problem aside. Again.

Whether it was the lurking panic, the filming disruption or my lack of sleep I didn't know, but I was suddenly starving. Today seemed to already have gone on twice as long as usual. Eating my sandwiches as I worked, I loaded up the first batch of thyme, steadying the bushes as I bumped the barrow down the shallow steps. Every bump released an aromatic cloud. It always amazed me how such tiny leaves could hold such a huge scent. I hefted the largest bush up and the smell surrounded me, it was in my nostrils, woven into my hair, on my skin. Sharp and long, piercing and somehow arrow-pure. Thyme was used as an antiseptic in olden times, long before they understood the science. Maybe that was why I associated it so strongly with health and vigour. If a marathon could have a defining herb, it would be thyme.

I arranged the plants on the spoke nearest the path, woody and ragged ones at the back, smaller ones at the front. The old gardeners would have created new bushes at regular intervals, layering or growing on cuttings as the plants were harvested and used up. I frowned, thinking of the rhyme I'd seen earlier.

Thyme on dial leads arrow straight . . .

The thing is, that was nonsense. It would change from year to year. Each of the spokes radiated out in a different direction. You'd need to know the planting plan the year it was written to solve the puzzle.

I went back up to the van to collect the clumps of rue. Rue was my least favourite herb. It was a valuable tool against headaches, and would most certainly have been used as such during the Great War, but the leaves brought me out in blisters. I pulled on elbow length gauntlets, sweating in them as I transported the swaddled bundles down to the bed. I placed them along the far spoke of the herb dial. They shouldn't be a problem there. I hammered a *Warning: Irritant* notice into the ground for good measure, just in case any of the crew got curious.

'How are you doing? Do you needed a hand?'

Theo stood behind me, proffering a bottle of water. I'd been concentrating so hard on not swiping myself with the rue that I hadn't heard him.

I peeled off the gauntlets and took a swig gratefully. 'Thanks. I'm roasting here. I can't believe you're wearing trousers, not shorts.'

'Don't possess any. Do you want any help carting your plants down?'

'No, thanks. I'm fine. These are all I brought for the moment. I'll dig them in, then go back for the rest once I've worked out what else is needed.' I considered the herb dial. I wouldn't need to bring lavender, sage or rosemary as they were here already, on the next level up. But they looked what they were — overgrown, straggly escapees. I could trim them, of course, but . . .

'I wonder if I can put a layer of gravel around the sage and the rosemary?' I said aloud. 'I don't know if it's period, but I'm thinking it would suppress the weeds and increase the dew-catching ability of the plot. It would tidy it too. It would make it look more as if it belonged to the herb dial below.'

Theo gave a short laugh. 'Tie the beds together, you mean? I agree, but you'll need to be sure. Bruce is rabid about historical accuracy.'

'I'll have the information somewhere. Gravel or shingle would be good. Then I can stand tubs of mint around to fill in the gaps. They'd add architecture to the bed as well as being useful.'

'Tubs?'

'I keep all my varieties in large earthenware pots at the nursery. It's far kinder to owners than leaving them with a bed full of invasive mint roots.'

Or I could just take the pots of mint back with me at the end of the shoot. I had a momentary pang, wondering what would happen to the bed once the TV crew had left. Technically, of course, once I had been paid for the plants, they were no longer mine — and most herbs can take an astonishing amount of neglect, as witness the old bushes still here — but it still hurt to think my new ones might be torn out and summer bedding put down instead.

'What's the matter?' said Theo.

I scowled. 'Just me being stupid, thinking about what's going to happen to the herb dial once filming has finished and the manor goes back to being a family house again.' But it *was* heart-twisting to nurture plants and grow them on and take care of them day in day out and then not be able to bring them to their full potential. 'Go on, upset me. What are the tenants like?'

Satisfaction crossed Theo's face. 'Gone,' he said.

I raised my eyebrows. 'That came from the heart. Were they bad neighbours? Coralie said they were difficult about letting the film crew on to the site. I can tell they weren't gardeners, judging by the shed not having been opened since seed packets were priced in pennies.'

'Tell me about it. They had contractors who brought everything in. Wansdale Manor has been on a long lease for years. The tenants didn't care about the garden, so long as they had complete privacy, hence all the security fencing. They won't be back. They were furious when the lease wasn't renewed and have bought somewhere else.'

'The next tenants might still trash the herb dial.' I tucked stray bits of hair inside my scarf as I thought aloud. 'Maybe if I put in labels they'll realise the plants are functional. I do realise not everyone sees quite as much beauty in a bunch of undistinguished shrubs as I do.'

He grinned. 'You're not a hard-nosed businesswoman at all, are you?'

He was a fine one to talk. I cast a meaningful look across the boundary at his own business. 'I'm a plantswoman,' I said. 'And right now I need to fetch cans so I can water this lot in as soon as I get them in the ground. I wonder if there's a standpipe? Otherwise I'll have to get it all from the house.' I looked around. 'The monks probably used the river. If I do the same, I'll end up falling in.'

Theo scuffed his boot along the earth by the side of the shed. 'The ground is firm here. I'd guess there would have been rainwater butts at one time, the same as I've got next to my barn. I'm pretty sure one of mine is original. Bruce raved over my barn. He decided straight away that he was going to film my sections there. We'd better ask the props team to provide us with matching WW1 watering cans so the continuity works.'

I nodded, gazing between the encroaching willows towards his barn. 'It's a pity the railings are so high between us. I could have just hopped over and fetched a pail. I can't even go along by the river because of all the brambles.'

Theo's tanned skin turned sallow in a split-second. His hands clenched. 'Don't . . . '

I barely had time to be astonished

before instinct took over and I was scooping up the nearest thyme bush. 'Bury your face in that,' I ordered. 'Take a deep breath. Sit down.'

He folded abruptly on to the step of the shed, breathing in the thyme. 'Thank you,' he said, his voice muffled. 'I'll be okay in a moment.'

I hesitated, torn between curiosity as to what the matter was and not wanting to pry. That had been awfully sudden. However, it was his business, not mine. His colour was coming back, so I left him to recover while I started planting the rue. After a few more minutes, I heard the thump of the bush being replaced.

'I'll sort you out a hose. I've got a long one next door.'

Watching him covertly as he headed for the house, I noticed the trace of a limp. Odd that I hadn't seen it before. Stop it, Jen. Concentrate on the herb dial. Get the plants in.

It didn't take long to do the two outer spokes. The thyme and the rue framed the bed nicely. After Theo had brought me the hose and I'd watered these first herbs in, I stood for quite a while looking from the bare ground to my sketch and back again, thinking about which plants to bring over next. For medicinal purposes, I would need feverfew, chamomile, calendula and valerian. I'd need comfrey and winter-green too, but I'd have to bring them over in my boggy containers. They'd never last in this dry, sunny soil. Wintergreen especially was a real challenge to site. With any luck, I'd be able to dig some in near the riverbank just for the filming.

For the table, they'd want marjoram, coriander and parsley. I could check with the strong-minded cook in the kitchen about that. It would also be worth asking Coralie if there were references to particular plants in the script that I hadn't already thought of. If so, I had better have them growing in or near the herb dial before Bruce swooped down on me with Fran in tow demanding to film the actress-Louise gathering them. I shut up the shed and headed for the house to find Coralie.

She was glued to Bruce's side. He was in a tight, earnest huddle with the cook and Coralie was making notes almost as fast as they were speaking. Evidently she was still devastated by his earlier disappointment in her when she'd failed to fetch me out of the research room fast enough. I hesitated, not knowing how long these things took. Ages, probably. If I went home now, I could load up the mint, grab something else to eat and ask her when I got back.

My indecision was interrupted by a text from Chris saying he was unexpectedly free, could be with me in ten minutes and would I like him to buy me lunch?

Sometimes, Chris came up with remarkably stupid questions.

★ ★ ★

I was braced for an inquisition, but although Chris did ask me nicely how the job was going and passed on an enquiry from Ewan on the state of my eviction order, it was clear he was really angling for a look around the manor as the price of free food. This was an occupational hazard of being the sister of an architect, but as he enthused over the building, it solved the riddle of why Wansdale had rung a bell at the back of my mind. It transpired that the manor was a significant medieval building, but no one had been able to gain access to it for years. Chris was almost drooling at the prospect of seeing inside.

I put my hunger on hold and took him towards the house. As ever, he was personable and charming with any crew we encountered and they were all so busy setting up for filming that no one seemed to mind us wandering around, provided we didn't get in the way. Chris loved the house. He adored the staircase and the gallery and happily explained the finer points of the construction to Fran's camera.

'He's not really here,' I told her. 'He's taking me to lunch.'

Fran filmed him being enthusiastic anyway, then went back to laying cables.

'Upstairs?' asked Chris. 'Just quickly?'

From the back of the house, I heard Bruce's voice. 'Come on then,' I said. Judging by Fran's reaction, once Bruce knew we had a proper architect on the premises, he'd think of a dozen things to ask him, whether it was in the original script or not. Organic, Coralie had called his way of working. It seemed to me that was just film-speak for making it up as you went along.

Quite frankly, after the magnificent Great Hall and the lovely terrace room, the bedrooms came as a disappointment. They had been modernised by the tenants, rendering them bland and featureless. Apart from the casements that Chris instantly swooped on with cries of delight, this room, for example, was a far cry from the one next door, currently being re-Edwardianised by the props team for use as documentary-Louise's bedroom.

Chris stopped taking photos of the shutters and glanced out of the window. 'My God,' he said. 'That looks like . . . no, no it can't be.'

'Can't be who?' I asked, coming over. I was intrigued. It was unusual for him to be less than laid back over anything except architecture.

Chris turned away from the window. 'It must be hunger making me light-headed. I thought I saw a chap I knew at Cambridge. Genius night-climber. Completely fearless.'

Night climbing was one of the activities Chris had chosen not to share with the family until after he had graduated, for which I was very grateful. Dad had quite enough to worry about with the weight of each and every one of his patients' problems on his shoulders. The thought that his youngest son was clambering happily across the roofs of Cambridge colleges in the evenings with only grippy-soled shoes as a safety aids would have done his blood pressure no good at all.

I peered out of the window, but saw nothing except the garden falling away in its lovely curves towards the river. The camera crew were now doing complicated things on the terrace. Bruce was pacing in front of them, firing notes at Coralie. Just visible next door, Theo was pushing a barrow load of shallow boxes into his barn, so he evidently *did* do some of his own work now and again. 'You can see the shape of the whole original garden from here,' I said. 'Isn't it lovely?'

Beyond Theo's barn was the remains of an old wisteria-clad wall. I wondered if that was where the kitchen garden used to be. The area seemed mostly populated by hens now. I also wondered if the gaps in the bricks were deliberate or the ravages of time. Maybe Theo needed the MovingInk money as much as I did.

'You and your piles of dirt,' teased Chris.

'You and your piles of stones,' I retorted. 'Can we get some food now,

111

please? If you've seen enough, that is?'

He threw me a grin. 'Fascinating house. I could spend a whole week here. I suppose the foxy blonde isn't single, is she?'

I glanced down. Coralie. I might have known. Chris had an eye for an elegant girl as well as an elegant building. He never stuck with any of them though. He drove Mum nuts because she'd no sooner filled in a mental index-card on one girlfriend than he'd said a regretfully charming goodbye to her and picked up with another. When questioned, he claimed they all had ulterior motives. He wanted a girl who liked him for himself rather than the trappings he brought with him.

'I don't know,' I said. 'If Coralie has got a partner, he must be remarkably understanding. She seems to work terrific hours, not to mention having a huge fangirl fixation on Bruce.'

'Pity.' But it seemed the attraction was mutual because when we crossed paths at the bottom of the stairs,

Coralie blinked and gave Chris a look equally as long as the one he'd given her.

'Ahem,' said Chris meaningfully to me.

I could take a hint. 'Coralie, this is my brother Chris. He's an architect specialising in historic buildings and is very interested in the manor. I hope it was okay to show him around?'

'Sure,' she said, their eyes still locked. 'Whenever you like. Here, have my card. It's got my email address on.'

I sighed. This happened every single time. I could see my lunch atomising while they danced around the first-contact preliminaries. Chris was already giving Coralie one of his own cards in exchange.

'Coralie,' called Bruce, coming into the hall from the back corridor. 'Find me Jen Herbs and . . . oh, there you are.' He looked at me accusingly, as if I shouldn't be out of my assigned space.

'I was just off to lunch and to fetch more plants,' I said. 'Did you want me for something?'

'The chat with the cook, Mrs Merryweather. It will have to be first thing in the morning. She's got equipment arriving later.'

I must have looked bewildered because he tutted impatiently.

'For the EPK,' he said. 'The segment where Mrs Merryweather tells you the herbs and seasoning she'll need. You'll have to have them in situ so we can film the gardener picking them. It's in the scene schedule Coralie gave you.'

Behind Bruce's shoulder, there was a look of appalled horror on Coralie's face. Poor girl. It was probably the first thing she'd forgotten to do in her entire life. Welcome to my world, girlfriend.

'Oh, right,' I said. 'Sorry, I haven't looked at that properly yet. I was concentrating on getting the herb dial dug and sorting out the right period feel for the design. Tomorrow morning is fine. Thanks for letting me know.'

'Mrs Merryweather is a considerable authority on historical cookery,' he added, as if I might shortchange her by sliding in inferior plants. 'Additionally, she has an Equity card, so she'll be playing the part of the cook in the documentary.' His attention switched to Chris. I could almost see him assessing him for screen presence and coming up with a winner.

Coralie rushed to redeem herself. 'Bruce, this is Jen's brother, Chris. He's a heritage architect.'

Bruce nodded, docketing the information. 'Could be useful. Appreciated.' He strode off.

'Thank you,' Coralie said to me in heartfelt tones. 'I'll email you the cutaway scenes right now.'

'We're off for a spot of late lunch,' said Chris. 'Care to join us?'

Coralie's eyes lit up, then she shook her head. 'Sorry, too busy.' She darted a quick look across the enormous hall to where Bruce was playing back one of the cameramen's footage. 'Um, Jen, could you do a massage again later? I won't make a habit of it, but it really did help.'

'Yes, of course.'

'Thanks.'

Chris bathed her in a warm smile. 'Jen's massages are famous in the family. She'd have been a celebrity sports physio by now if she hadn't switched to herbs.'

'Food,' I repeated, and steered him outside towards the cars. He was a good brother, but like the rest of the family, he did tend to put more emphasis on success than I thought necessary.

7

After we'd eaten, Chris helped load my big tubs of mint into the back of his 4x4. We returned to Wansdale just as Theo emerged from the turreted garage, hauling an old pony trap of all things.

Chris's jaw went slack. 'It *is* you! Theo Grainger! I thought you went to Europe. What are you doing here?'

Theo shrugged, outwardly easy but there was defensive steel in every line of him. 'Heritage vegetables, mostly. Would you like a weekly box? A fiver to you. Mate's rates.'

'Vegetables! But you . . . I mean . . . You were . . . '

I was enjoying this. It wasn't often I saw Chris lost for words. 'You'll have to excuse my brother,' I said to Theo. 'He's only recently learned how to string a sentence together.'

Chris made a swatting movement.

'Theo, you graduated top of your year. With honours, prizes, job offers tumbling into your lap. I mean, we heard you had a fall, but . . . '

'Yeah, well. How are you doing, Chris? Who are you working for these days? Have you seen over the manor? Right up your street, isn't it?'

It was enough to divert Chris. I unloaded my tubs of mint while they talked architecture, then kissed him goodbye. 'Thanks for the meal,' I called as he drove away.

Theo was still standing next to the tubs of mint. I didn't give the silence time to fall. 'He's not subtle, my brother, but he understands the value of a decent lunch. I could move mountains now. Funny, you two knowing each other.'

Theo steadied my small trolley. 'Do you want a hand?'

I met his eyes directly. 'Only if you want to lend one. Otherwise I'm fine.' I rubbed one of the leaves. 'Applemint. Isn't it fabulous?'

His smile was a little strained. 'It is.

Thank you. And thank you again for the thyme earlier.'

I twiddled my fingers at him. 'Go on, back to work with you. Where did the pony trap come from? Bruce will adore it. I'd leave it there if I were you. Judging by what they are doing with Louise's bedroom upstairs, the props team will have it sanded down and two coats of paint applied by this time tomorrow.'

Down at the herb dial, I heaved the last pot into place. I was going to be so fit once this job was finished. Either fit or in an early grave, one of the two. I sat on the step of the shed for a moment to recover. Sunlight danced past the doorframe into the dim interior. If this shed was mine, I'd have the willows down in a trice to make it a useable workspace again. I could feel it whispering blandishments at me.

'Stop it,' I told it. 'I've got a job to do.' All the same, I continued to sit there, half-in and half-out of the past, picturing the whole garden as it might have been a hundred years ago.

This would never do. I stood again and as I did, my eye was caught by a knothole in the rafters. A knothole? In such an impeccably crafted shed? I caught my breath and reached up.

And touched the key to the little writing desk, cunningly set into the wood. Hidden in plain sight.

Heart thumping, I fetched the desk out, set it on the bench, turned the key and lifted the sloped lid. The diary lay on top, thrust in carelessly which was why the first page had come adrift. It fell open when I picked it up. *Oh, Robbie*, I read. *Oh Robbie, my love.*

There was a footfall on the path outside. I dropped the diary back, hurriedly shut the lid and locked it. My hands were shaking so much I could barely hold the key.

'Um, Jen . . . ?'

I looked out into the late afternoon sun, dazzled and disorientated.

Coralie stood on the path, slightly embarrassed. 'My neck. Could you?'

I swallowed. 'Yes, of course. I'm about finished here for the moment. I need to load up more plants at home.' I slipped the writing desk into my satchel, closed the shed and followed her up to the house. I could feel the desk bumping against my hip but there was no way I could leave it here tonight. Neither it nor the diary inside.

'I thought the kitchen, if you don't mind? Mrs Merryweather's gone home. Sorry about messing up your timings tomorrow, but she's fearfully expensive. We were lucky to secure her. Fortunately, she's worked with Bruce before.'

'Ah, the massage, good,' said Bruce, hurrying in. 'Coralie says you have certificates. Is that right?'

I blinked. 'Yes, but . . . '

'Excellent. Now, in the scene we are thinking of, a patient's injured leg goes into spasms and Louise eases the pain with lavender cream. Can you do that? The massage?'

'Well, yes, but I . . . '

'I know, I know. We only contracted

you to do the herbs. We'll amend that. We will need you to make the lotion and say a few words about it. Coralie's sent you the reference, yes? If you can also explain the massage technique, it not only saves us getting someone in just for one or two scenes, it gives more cohesion to the project as a whole.'

'I . . . I suppose . . . '

'Good. Sit down at the table under the light, Coralie. For now, Jen, I want to see how your hands move. It'll be a nice touch in the EPK. 'During preparations, the production coordinator suffered from neck strain, and it was discovered that Jen Matlock was a skilled masseuse as well as a herbalist.' Fran, I want a long shot, then close-up on Jen's hands. Okay, go.'

I looked reproachfully at Coralie as she pulled a chair to the indicated space.

'Sorry,' she whispered. 'I know you don't like being filmed, but it will tie things together marvellously and my neck really could do with it.'

'Come on then.' I tuned out Fran and Bruce and called on my inner senses to feel Coralie's neck. I was amazed when the first whiff of lavender oil relaxed her. Amazed and a little bit guilty. A trigger just from one session? Heavens, she was suggestible. I'd better warn her never to let anyone hypnotise her. From my point of view, it was great to find her not nearly as taut as the day before. There was still a mid-level anxiety running right through her, but I suspected she wouldn't lose that until we'd finished the filming.

She stretched luxuriously once I'd finished. 'Thanks, that's wonderful. I'm sending out for pizza. Do you want some?'

'Yes, she does,' answered Theo, crossing to the sink and filling the kettle. 'I can tell that just by looking at her.'

Coralie hurried down to the other end of the kitchen after Bruce. I slid into the chair she'd vacated to sit down for a few minutes before I headed home. 'I am here, you know,' I said.

'And unable to speak for yourself. You don't fool me. That massage took it out of you.'

'It's been a long day,' I hedged, 'but if one of those mugs is mine, I wouldn't say no. Where did you spring from?'

He leaned against the worktop, waiting for the kettle to boil. 'Been here a while. I was watching you work. I could feel you caring. Have you trained?'

A defensive prickle skittered across my skin. 'I know what I'm doing, if that's what you mean. I'm aware which muscles go where and do what.' Then, under his neutral gaze, I capitulated. Checking Bruce and Fran were safely huddled over the camera footage out of earshot, I muttered, 'If you must know, I started a physio degree and had to stop.'

Theo dropped his voice likewise. 'Why? You looked like a natural.'

'That's just it,' I said, keeping a wary eye on the others. 'Don't say anything to Coralie, but if I think about the theory when I'm manipulating muscles or setting breaks, I can't do it. The external diagrams stop me feeling with my fingers what's wrong. I couldn't take the risk of losing that so I dropped out. Stuck with first aid and switched to herbs instead. Can we change the subject now?'

Theo was quiet for the longest moment, long enough for me to wonder why I'd opened up to him like that. I hardly even knew him and I wasn't at all sure I trusted him. Maybe it was because he too worked with his hands. He understood land memory. He was, I don't know, flexible of mind.

'I climb like that, or I used to,' he said at last. 'My hands and feet connect with the building. My body knows how to stretch to get all of me up to this window ledge, or across that gap. I don't have to tell it anything. Sometimes, though, I've studied the architecture in advance and then if I start superimposing what my brain remembers over what my fingers *know*, it all goes horribly wrong.'

'All good,' said Bruce, striding the

length of the kitchen. 'Coralie, update Jen's schedule.' He swept out, followed by his retinue.

Theo made the tea and sat down with me at the table. He took a shallow breath. 'That's why . . . that's how I fell.'

'Fell?'

'Chris mentioned it earlier. He doesn't get any more tactful, does he?'

'It's not one of his major strengths, no.'

'Stupid of me not realising you might be related. Matlock isn't that common a name.'

'It's not that uncommon either. I don't see why you'd make the connection. You knew Chris at university. At that time he still lived in Edgware with the family. Here we are in Shropshire. Nobody would connect us from that. I don't even look like him. Granny reckons Dad and I are throwbacks to her prairie forbears. Was it a bad fall, then?'

'Bad?' He gave an unamused laugh

and rolled up his trouser leg. 'Yes, if you call thirty feet on to spiked railings bad. What you said this morning brought it back, hence the faintness. I needed eighty stitches, thigh to ankle. I was sent home too soon, the wound burst, got infected, finally healed. This is a small sample, okay? There's a reason I don't wear shorts in the summer.'

Eighty stitches? I stared at the lower part of his scar, nausea rising in my throat, then abruptly rushed to the loo. 'Sorry,' I said when I returned to the kitchen.

Theo was cradling his mug. I don't think he'd moved, except to roll the trouser down again. 'My fault for inflicting it on you,' he said, his voice stiff. 'I apologise. It's not a pretty sight.'

'Don't be ridiculous. I could cope with the sight,' I replied tartly. 'I'm not squeamish. I don't find the scar ugly or distasteful. But I could feel the mangling your calf and thigh muscles have been through. The calf is worst, isn't it? No wonder you limp occasionally.'

It was his turn to stare at me. 'You know that from one brief glance? You *felt* that? Without even touching me?'

I buried my nose in the steam from my tea. 'Yes, well. There's a reason I'm a gardener, not a physiotherapist.'

⋆   ⋆   ⋆

What with the pizza and the tea, it was later than I hoped by the time I got home. My body was crying out for bed, preferably until this time tomorrow. Instead, I made strong coffee, dealt with my post, answered emails, filled the outstanding orders and lined everything up ready to be packed and posted tomorrow. It was all necessary work, but I knew what I was really doing was procrastinating. Under my surface busyness, Theo's injuries were still there, a nightmare lodged in my synapses. I had never felt somebody else's damage so strongly, not even when Chris fell out of the apple tree and broke two bones in his leg. I'd had to sit on him then to stop him writhing while I set and splinted his leg, but it had still been a cleaner pain than the sluggish, malevolent sense of sheer wrongness in Theo's calf.

Tired as I was, I had to shake the horror of that mangling or I'd never sleep. I needed to get back to equilibrium. The best way to achieve it was to lose myself completely. A book? Music? An obscure treatise on medieval herb beds that I would need to concentrate on?

Ah, I could look up the historical use of gravel in gardens. Google never slept. I rubbed my eyes and refreshed my email inbox. Coralie's scene sheet popped up. Even better.

I pulled a pad towards me to make notes. Once I knew what I would definitely need in the herb dial, I could cross check against my list of herbal remedies of the 1900s and see which other plants I could fit into the space.

There were to be several medical scenes. General cleaning and binding of wounds. The leg massage on a Lt Wright that Bruce had already mentioned. There was also an eye-bath, infusions to bring down fevers from infections contracted on the battlefield, something to calm a shell-shock patient and a salve of some sort was required to smooth all over one Corporal Ginger Gibbs who was covered with an angry raised rash. I scrolled back to the massage scene. Apparently Lt Wright was an amputee, but Bruce didn't think we'd need quite that level of verisimilitude. I stared at that sentence for quite a few moments, then blanked it out of my head for the sake of my own sanity. I would look up massage for amputees so I could drop a couple of knowledgeable facts into the commentary. There would be a website somewhere with the history of topical treatment. Reading on through the medical scenes, it appeared Lt Wright would be fitted with a wooden leg by the end of the programme. Presumably they'd already sourced someone from the army medical corps who was an expert on historical prosthetics. False legs were definitely not in my remit.

I made notes, jotted down some lines of inquiry and finally felt calm enough to go to bed. I'd just pulled the sheet up to my chin when I remembered the writing desk. The one with the diary inside. And now I had a dilemma. From the single sentence I'd glimpsed — *Oh, Robbie. Oh Robbie, my love* — the diary contained feelings that the writer had never intended to be made public. On the other hand, if that writer was Louise, the diary might also have all the herbal details I needed. I was pretty sure what would have been used for eye-baths and rashes, but that wasn't likely to be good enough in Bruce's book. He wanted accuracy.

It was really late by now, but the thought of the amount of research time I could save by reading Louise's own notes propelled me back downstairs to my satchel. I'd also be interested for myself, to see if there were any remedies we'd lost over time which I could make today for Wild About Herbs. I carried the writing slope up to bed with a sense of cautious anticipation. The loose first page of the diary had said that at last she had found a refuge. I turned the key in the lock, lifted out the hundred-year-old book and read the second page.

I have discussed with Brown the changes in our planting. More comfrey will certainly be needed, so he must stop pulling it up from the water's edge. I have gravely agreed with him that so many plants en masse look untidy, and I have shaken my head in sympathy over the necessity for them, but the country folk call comfrey 'knitbone' for good reason. I believe the coming months will prove its worth. Feverfew is also likely to be necessary, so we must endure its aggressive nature and unpleasant odour, and I must try to extend the wintergreen patch under the willow as well. In truth, mass planting like this, with no need for tidiness and constant weeding, is a blessing. Brown's knees trouble him in old age. Less physical work means he can supervise from his cottage and leave me with the run of the shed. He grumbles, but it is Wansdale's duty, given the wounded soldiers we will be sent. The thought that I can help them, that I can do something, is the only thing keeping me here and not heading for the nurse's training school in London. I just pray I can help these injured men, and that Freddy and Edmund are never amongst them.

The hospital beds are in place now in all the downstairs rooms, the permanent nurses and first patients arrive tomorrow. In a strange way I am looking forward to it. Between the nursing and the garden I can escape Geraldine's impertinence and Mother's busy plans for my future. Edmund's children are sweet, but I never thought to hate a sister-in-law as much as I do

Geraldine. Now I will only have to endure her smugness and self-sacrificial air at mealtimes. One finds small mercies where one can.

The page was tiny, the writing small and neat. The sight of Louise's words, and those words themselves bringing her vividly to life, affected me more than I had expected. She had already helped me by mentioning comfrey, feverfew and wintergreen — so evidently it *would* grow here — now I flicked through further entries, looking for references to specific herbs.

The injuries are horrific, much worse that anything I could ever have imagined. The men are in shock, in constant pain. Some scream and some bear it, grateful to be alive. Three soldiers came in today, all from the same company. Captain and Lieutenant Wright (brothers) and an ordinary soldier who joined up with them from their estate. The older brother has a broken leg and arm, the younger has lost one leg below the knee. His wound is still raw and had been disturbed on the journey, so I immediately applied honey and a dressing, which seemed to afford him some relief. I learned that the company were bombarded by artillery. Captain Wright was hit and Lieutenant Wright fell off the duck boards into the mud, screaming with pain. Corporal Gibbs lay down with no thought to his own safety and hauled him out, for all he was injured himself, and then carried him to the First Aid post before going back to help Captain Wright. Captain Wright says he saved his brother's life, for the younger man would never have got out of the mud alone and would probably have drowned in it. That is why he insisted Corporal Gibbs accompany them here to recuperate, though he is only an NCO not a full officer.

I kept my finger in the page, considering. Lt Wright was the amputee in the scene schedule. I wondered if Louise might have written about massaging his leg in the diary. Where had Bruce got the information from anyway? He was far too wedded to authenticity to have made the scenes up. Hospital records? No, I remembered now. Coralie had mentioned soldiers' letters. I'd have to ask her. I yawned. The writing was getting difficult to read. I flicked through some more entries. Ah, here we were.

Lieutenant Wright is more comfortable today. He has been having increasingly severe spasms, so I rubbed comfrey cream into his leg while Corporal Gibbs sat by him talking over old times. They are neither of them very old, and grew up together on their estate, though in different spheres. They are like Freddy and Edmund, like so many here, young men who have become old too fast with all they have seen. At any rate, Corporal Gibbs kept him distracted while I worked, which was a good thing. It is strange, but I could sense Lt Wright's missing leg and could not seem to stop the massage until I had eased the pain still writhing in him from its loss. From what they were saying, the lieutenant had planned to go to Cambridge, but the war put an end to it. He is quieter and more reflective than his brother. So many of the injured men here are not in the least military-like and are only doing their duty to this country as best they know how. As one, they all want to turn back the clock and return the world to peace. Lt Wright says that will never be possible now. Even in this short time, the men who have gone away have changed. The women who were left behind have changed. I know I have. I cannot imagine returning to the life I had before. My horizons are wider. Lt

Wright agrees. He says when the war is over, we must all make our lives afresh. He has great dreams. I do not think the loss of his leg will stop him.

As happens so often after spending time with the patients, I was dropping with tiredness when my shift was over. Corporal Gibbs saw it and offered to carry my basket down to the shed so I could replenish supplies. I think he secretly lusts after the shed for he is a carpenter in ordinary life, but perhaps I wrong him. He stayed outdoors for the rest of the afternoon and helped to harvest more comfrey. We use such a lot of it, I am thankful it does so well here. He said standing up to his ankles in our river was a thousand lifetimes away from the mud of the trenches and will give him a tranquil memory to take back. He speaks practically and without regret and quietly does what he can to fix things. I like him very much. Lt Wright is lucky to have such a friend.

Louise wasn't the only tired herbalist here. My eyes were giving up the struggle to remain open. I closed my hand around the diary and slept.

8

What I really wanted to do next was to read the whole diary, but a rush of Wild About Herbs orders combined with the documentary work kept me busy for very nearly more hours than there were in the day. The red eviction notice slid further and further down my ToDeal-With pile. Towards the end of the week, however, I'd cleared my backlog, finished the herb dial and was almost, *almost*, becoming accustomed to cameras swooping on me at any moment and Bruce firing questions at me. Coralie explained earnestly that this was part of his organic approach and that it gave the programme energy. I reserved judgement on that. It still looked more to me as if he was inventing the documentary on the hoof. He was the same with everyone except Mrs Merryweather, whom he approached, as the whole film crew did, with wary homage. I found this quite funny. My only interaction with the heritage cook had been to look though her list of herbs and say cheerfully that there wasn't anything on it not in my bedding plan already. She had run my sample leaves through her fingers and murmured that she *usually* used her own supplier but my plants were of an acceptable standard. I smiled and replied it was just as well since the viewer would have seen them picked not two minutes before she started cooking with them.

Coralie regarded me with a kind of awe as Mrs M and I exchanged professional nods before I went back out to the garden. Then again, she hadn't spent twenty-six years dealing with my mother.

'The bed is looking good,' said Theo, stopping by on his way down to the river. He was wearing thigh-waders and being trailed by a cameraman, so I assumed he was being an expert and about to demonstrate how something or other would be done in 1915.

'Thank you,' I said. I still wasn't sure what to think about him. He seemed to be around a lot more than someone simply providing heritage vegetables should be, and was at once familiar yet distant with the TV crew. Earlier this week I'd opened up the shed to find a man's boot prints on the floor and evidence that the contents had been disturbed. For no reason whatsoever, I knew it had been Theo. He couldn't believe the Wansdale Bounty was hidden in the shed, surely?

Now I gestured to the bucket in his hand. 'Are you fish-man as well as heritage-veg-man?'

He shot me a look. 'Don't give them ideas. I'm river-silt-as-mulch-man today. Care to join us?'

'Not a chance. Although . . . ' I eyed his waders speculatively. 'I don't suppose you'd like to plant me some comfrey while you're messing around on the bank? The plants need to go in at the water's edge. The manor would have had a great swathe of it a century ago.'

Behind him, the cameraman nodded with enthusiasm. Fran, who had been dismantling her static camera, stiffened in alert terrier mode.

'Might as well,' said Theo. 'But you owe me. Have you got it ready?'

'You will? You hero.' I quickly crossed to the trough by the shed that the scene dressers had presented me with, and loaded my barrow with half a dozen well-grown baskets before he could change his mind. Unsurprisingly, all the comfrey that had been by the river margins in Louise's day had long since been pulled up in the interests of tidiness. I'd been putting off replacing them until I'd got the herb dial sorted out, so was delighted now to merely trundle them down to the marshy bank and then point to show Theo where I'd like them sunk in the mud.

'They would be easier to plant down here where I am,' remarked Theo, after first dredging up his bucketful of silt.

'But if I've got to harvest them in a fortnight for the camera, I have to be able to reach them,' I said.

He chuckled and I realised, astonishingly, that he was winding me up. He clambered half way up the bank, plied my spade expertly and plunged the comfrey plants into the damp soil. 'Better check you can reach them.'

I edged forward, stretching as if to twist off one of the leafy stems. Just in time I saw him reach teasingly for my arm. I pulled it back sharpish.

Unbalanced, he slipped in the mud, floundering awkwardly sideways as his footing gave way and he landed with an ungainly splash.

'Theo!' I rushed towards him, feeling mud ooze around my ankles and grip my boots. Stretching down, I grabbed one of his arms with both my hands and hauled. With my leverage he managed to find purchase for his boots and heaved himself up the bank. 'Serves me right for being idle,' I called, squelching across for my abandoned

144

spade. 'I'm now far muddier than I would have been if I'd sunk the baskets myself.' I turned and looked at him cheerfully, but his face was distorted with pain. 'Theo?' I asked. 'What's up?'

'I'll just bet there used to be a jetty here,' he said through clenched teeth. 'I think I found the remains of it.'

I glanced down at his leg and gasped in horror. One wader was ripped and blood was oozing out, mixing garishly with river mud. 'Theo! That's your bad leg, isn't it? I need to get it clean. Can you walk on it?'

'Just,' he said. His face was grey. 'It feels as if it's near the old scar. Go on then. What would Louise do now if it was one of the patients down here?'

'Honey,' I said without hesitation. 'It's antiseptic. She'd slap honey on the wound straight away and bind it up, maybe bruising a couple of wintergreen leaves into the mixture for good measure. Trouble is, I don't have any honey. Of course, if you're dead-set on recreating the past, we could try using cobwebs? I've got loads in the shed and they're packed with penicillin. Or,' I added with heavy irony, 'I can slice the wader off, clean you up, patch the cut temporarily and get you to the surgery!'

'I have honey,' said Theo. 'I even have WW1 bee houses. Help me around to my side of the garden and you can put some on direct from the hive.'

I gaped. 'You're not serious?'

'Watch me. Bruce will love it.'

'He will!' agreed Theo's cameraman, still filming us.

'Bloody right,' muttered Fran, pulling out her mobile with her free hand, presumably to let the director know.

'This is ridiculous,' I said as we tugged our feet clear of the mud with a set of horrible sucking noises. 'You need a doctor.'

'You don't trust your remedies?'

'Of course I trust them. But I'm only a first-aider and that leg looks serious. It's going to need more than a dressing.' I risked a look down. Blood was still welling out of the mess. 'Oh, come on then. Use my shoulder to balance. Never mind the mud. It'll wash off.' Cursing the railings between the gardens, I helped him up through the terraced levels, grabbed my pack from the shed and paused by my boggy containers to nip off a couple of wintergreen leaves. Then we carried on across the back of the manor and into his property next door. All the way, I could feel what it was costing him. We picked up a small retinue, including a predictably enthusiastic Bruce, but I don't think Theo even noticed. He was stubborn, I'll give him that. He was limping badly and I knew it was dreadfully painful, but all his swearing was done sotto voce.

The top of Theo's market garden was beautifully neat. Tidy beds of serried vegetables all running down to the remains of the old wall. The wall itself, as I had seen from the upstairs window in the manor, had a pattern of gaps in the bricks.

'Breeze holes,' ground out Theo

when he saw me looking. 'Have you never come across them? They let the wind through in a controlled fashion instead of it curling over the top in force and knocking everything down. Through the gate there, that's where the hives are. They've been there forever. You'll excuse me while I tell them what's going on. It's a bee thing.'

I steadied him while he unlatched the gate and looked around as he lowered himself with a small escaped grunt of pain on to a wooden bench on the other side of the wall. There was an old-fashioned, long wooden cupboard next to him that had once been painted bright green, but had weathered over the years. Various remarkably pretty chickens were pecking around, golden ones, dark red ones, feathery-legged ones and adorable mop-headed punk ones. At our entrance, they bustled over hopefully. Theo scooped a handful of feed from a covered bin next to the bench and threw it on the ground to loud chirrups of satisfaction. Swathes of lilac wisteria tumbled across the top of the wall to complete what have been an idyllic picture if it hadn't been for the blood running sluggishly down Theo's calf.

'Lie down,' I said. 'I want that leg horizontal.' I braced myself to pull the remains of the wader off. His jeans were beyond repair so I hacked the material off at the knee with my knife.

'Fell,' he said, apparently to the bees buzzing overhead. 'My own fault. Showing off.' He squinted along the length of his body towards his leg and winced. 'Water butt,' he added, nodding to one side.

I'd already seen it. I sidestepped the hens, dipped a can and washed the gash, carefully trickling rosemary water from my pack over it afterwards as a disinfectant.

'Words,' Fran reminded me. I glared and repeated the actions, with dialogue.

Theo's eyes were closed now. 'Do you suppose when we're old and grey, we'll continue to explain our every

149

action to an invisible camera?'

'You're never going reach the old and grey stage if we don't get this wound closed up. The septicaemia will have finished you off long beforehand.'

He smiled faintly. 'Honey in the cupboard.'

That smile was a total killer. At a guess, it went with the man he'd been before he had the fall that had given him eighty stitches and a recluse complex. I fought down the sudden lurch in my chest and opened one of the doors in the weathered cupboard. A flake of emerald green paint floated to the ground. Inside, jars of clear amber honey glowed like jewels. 'You're sure about this?' I asked.

He didn't open his eyes. 'Are you?'

'Sure as anything.' It was true. I was sure. It was also true that I hadn't actually used honey on an injury myself, most of my first-aid patients preferring their cuts anointed with something out of a tube with a chemist's label on the box. Theo didn't need to know that though. What I did have was the memory of Louise's diary entry. I rapidly rinsed the wintergreen, ripped the leaves across and mashed them ferociously with a spoonful of honey in my miniature mortar, then I concentrated on holding Theo's calf firmly, smoothing the honey along it and using lint and linen strips from my pack to keep the wound closed once I was done. As I worked, explaining the process to the camera, Theo quietened.

'That's better,' he said at last. 'Thank you.'

I dropped to the sunbaked ground and leaned against the bench. 'I hope you got all that,' I said to Fran, 'because I'm not doing it again for anybody.'

Fran's fellow cameraman winked at me. 'Bruce will let you know. Why didn't the wintergreen smell like the stuff I had rubbed on my chest as a kid? I'm sure that's what Mum called it.'

'That would be US wintergreen. *Gaultheria*. Different shrub completely with a minty, aromatic scent. This is

English wintergreen, *Pyrola rotundifolia*. Good for wounds, germs, fevers, the lot.'

They left. Theo and I continued to rest. Chickens pecked around us, four or five of the red and gold punk ones fluttering up to where Theo was stretched out on the bench. It was, I think, the moment when I accepted Theo was one of the good guys. It's virtually impossible to harbour distrustful thoughts about someone who lets scruffy wind-up chickens roost on his chest.

Bees moved in and out of the hives. I followed their progress as I summoned the wherewithal to move. They came from all directions, some from the river, some from the vegetable beds, some from the main garden, taking advantage of the wind-holes in the old wall rather than flying over the top. 'We'd better call the surgery,' I said at last. 'You'll need stitches or steri-strips. The practice nurse will have a fit when she sees the dressing.'

'It feels fine at the moment. Clean. Cleaner than the original cut.'

'Theo, this isn't 1915. I may make a living out of complimentary medicine, but I would never claim it can do everything. As soon as you start moving, that gash is going to open up.'

'Yes, matron,' he said. He felt along the bench, dislodged a chicken and passed me the jar of honey. 'Have a spoonful for energy. You've wiped yourself out.'

'Just the adrenalin leaving.' But I hauled myself up and got another spoon out of the battered tin in the cupboard. The honey was warm and golden, tinged with thyme and bursting with life-affirming sweetness in my mouth. 'Awesome,' I murmured, shutting my eyes and letting the hot sun reinvigorate me. 'I should get back to work.'

'Sit here for a moment first. Stroke one of the Orpingtons. What you just did was pretty intense.'

'Which are the Orpingtons?'

'The gold-laced ones. They're very patient. Listen, what we were saying the other day, about how you instinctively know where to massage in order to relax muscles and put them back they way they should be.'

I tensed. 'Yes?'

'Jen, I could *feel* my leg mending as you smoothed the honey on. I could *feel* the torn blood vessels becoming less outraged at being ripped apart. I could feel the wound closing. I don't think it's going to open up again. It wouldn't dare.'

'You are so in shock,' I said. 'Get yourself a hot sweet tea and take whatever painkiller you usually have. See you later. And ring the surgery, okay?'

I let myself out through the gate. The hens clustered around Theo. Above me the bees lazily buzzed down from over the roof of the house and into their hives.

★ ★ ★

154

I got a call from Chris as I was walking back to the herb dial, telling me he might have found some land for me to rent.

'Thanks, Chris,' I said, 'but I'm really shattered. Can you email me the details? I'll make an appointment.'

'It's not far. I could pick you up from there and take you this afternoon?'

I knew what this was about. He wanted an excuse to come over and impress Coralie with his concerned brother act. 'Okay,' I said, too weary to argue. 'Ring me when you get here.'

The visit didn't take long. Chris delivered me back to the kitchen of Wansdale Manor where I offered him a coffee. Various crew members were perched around the table, including Theo. I was astonished to see him there, but glad he had the sense not to be doing any heavy digging just yet. However, from the way he was tucking into MovingInk's buttered toast without once glancing at the clock, I guessed he wasn't taking his injured leg to evening surgery any time soon.

'Looks good,' commented Chris, nodding towards the far end of the kitchen which had been completely Edwardianised by now.

'Where did they get that cooker?' I asked, gaping at the ugly upright monstrosity that had appeared since the morning. 'I thought Granny's was ancient, but this one looks incredibly old. Does it work?'

'It had better,' said Coralie, going pale at the thought that it might not. 'It's the one Mrs Merryweather specified. It costs a fortune to hire.'

Chris was fascinated by it. 'What make is it? I've taken several old stoves out of period kitchens, but never one like that. We sell them to vintage suppliers.'

Coralie's gaze instantly switched to Chris. 'Do you? That could be useful. Do you mind if we contact you from time to time?'

'Nothing I'd like more,' said my brother, smiling into her eyes.

Oh, give me strength. I crossed to Theo to see if there was any spare toast, but Bruce suddenly powered through the door, interrupting us.

'Coralie, I'm away for the evening. I've emailed you those disclaimers to send out.' And he was gone.

Coralie stared at the closing door, her face a crumpled mix of astonishment and sheer terror.

'What's the matter?' I asked.

She turned an abandoned puppy look on me. 'Something's wrong. Bruce never takes any time off during a shoot. Never. It's me. He's going to fire me. He must be interviewing for replacements.'

'What? Why would he do that?' said Chris. By his side, he twiddled his fingers at me in a family back-me-up gesture.

Her voice wobbled. 'I've made a couple of slips. I've disappointed him. You have to dedicate yourself utterly to any of Bruce's projects. That *must* be it. Why else would he take an evening off?'

'Lots of reasons,' said Chris bracingly. 'Someone's birthday? Summoned to the family home? A lead on another programme that might or might not come off? Don't beat yourself up. Even I can tell what a fantastic job you do, and that's without Jen confirming it.' His fingers twiddled at me even more urgently. *Give me something. Anything.*

Coralie stretched her mouth into an anguished smile. 'Thank you. I know I must seem needy and feeble, but MovingInk is my dream job. It means so much to me and it's totally the business on my CV, but it won't be worth anything without Bruce's recommendation, no matter how long I've been working for him.' Her voice rose.

'I was going to ask you, Coralie,' I said casually, reaching into my pack, 'I've been wondering about developing this as a perfume. What do you think?' I put the tiniest dab of lavender oil on her wrist and wafted it under her nose.

'Oh. Oh, that's lavender, isn't it? It's

lovely. I'd buy it.' She almost visibly relaxed in front of our eyes. 'How would you do it? In a bottle or as a spray?'

'Perfume stick probably, the packaging is less expensive.' Damn, now I'd probably find myself committed to it. As if I didn't have enough to do already. 'Theo, is there any more toast? I'm starving.'

'Oh, yes, food,' said Coralie, looking vaguely around the kitchen.

'Actually,' said Chris with a winning smile, 'I was going to take Jen out for a pub meal. Would you like to join us? And you too, Theo.'

Coralie bit her lip. 'Oh, no, I couldn't . . . '

'You could, you know,' I pointed out. 'Bruce isn't going to need you for taking notes and sending emails tonight. Think of it as replenishing your energy levels.' Yes, I was being nice and I honestly *did* think she needed to relax, but mostly this was the first I'd heard of a dinner invitation and it would almost certainly vanish again if Coralie decided to be self sacrificial and stay in her room to go over her production schedule for the three thousandth time.

'Well, it's very kind ... yes, yes please, I will.'

'Excellent,' said Chris. 'Theo?'

Theo evidently really did know Chris of old. He'd been watching the exchange with an appreciative expression. 'I'd be delighted to. As you can probably tell, I've run out of bread next door and the local pub does decent meals. Can you give me a lift, Jen? I can walk back.'

'You'll do no such thing,' I said. 'I'll run you home again afterwards. Doctor's list full this evening, was it?'

'I may have forgotten to ring.'

Chris wandered off with Coralie to fetch her accoutrements. It was a technique he'd mastered years ago, the casual assumption that he in some way now had the right to. I watched, slightly worriedly. I must tell him not to hurt her. There were a lot more insecurities under that poised city-girl surface than you'd expect.

'Are you going to need more lavender?' asked Theo.

I whirled around. 'How did you know what I was thinking?'

He looked amused. 'You are so transparent. Have you always acted first and thought later?'

'Story of my life. I didn't calm Coralie down just for Chris to take advantage of her though. I'll have a word with him at the pub.'

Theo's brow wrinkled. 'He was quite serious about a girl at uni. Did that peter out?'

'It's news to me. I didn't think he'd ever been serious. Mum despairs of him. That's why I don't want him to let Coralie down.'

'Does she despair of you too?'

'All the time. Oh . . . ' I saw what he meant, and blushed. 'No, not in that way. I don't have time for entanglements.' Although, to be fair to Mum, I don't think she ever expects blokes to fall for me anyway. Not ones who can speak in words of more than two syllables.

Dinner went surprisingly well. I'd half expected Theo and Chris to slip into the sort of erudite university banter that sometimes made Chris and his friends sound as if they were talking a different language. Theo, interestingly, wasn't having any of it. He talked like an ordinary person, like my oldest brother Ewan. I liked him the better for it.

Coralie was also interesting. Whether it was the lingering effects of the lavender or the sense of being off the leash for the evening, she was less all-consumed by the business of filming and was happy to talk about normal things like books and travelling. Oh, and Mother and the house in St John's Wood and the tedious, brainless society set that she'd escaped from as soon as she could, but then I'd gathered that. All was fine, in fact, until she remembered her beautiful manners and said, 'How was the site you saw this afternoon, Jen? Any good?'

I shrugged awkwardly. 'Nice size, but not suitable as a long term prospect. It faced north, which is why the rent was so low. I need south facing for the herbs. Thanks for the suggestion, anyway, Chris. I do appreciate you, even if I don't always show it.'

'I thought you ran Wild About Herbs from home,' said Theo with a frown.

'She's about to be evicted in the interests of a neighbourhood supermarket,' said Chris.

'Never mind me. I'll find somewhere. When are you going to ring the clinic, Theo?'

But if I could change the subject, he could change it back again. 'I'll do it in the morning. Jen, this is important. What about your plants? You must have a fair-sized plot. Where will you go?'

'I don't know,' I said flippantly. 'You know anyone with an acre or so of rubbish, south-facing land to spare?'

'Only Wansdale,' said Theo. 'You could use the rest of the garden. There's enough of it, and I saw the initial footage of you telling Fran the situation was perfect.'

'Oh do be serious, Theo. Of course

it's bloody perfect, but I need a permanent solution. The documentary is going to be finished in a couple of months and then the manor will be let again and I'll have to move everything just as it's got established.'

'The manor won't be let if it can be financed in some other way,' said Theo. 'I'd be happy not to have tenants in there at all.' He nodded at Coralie. 'Hiring Wansdale to MovingInk has been a revelation. There must be more opportunities like this one, don't you think?'

'Absolutely,' said Coralie. 'It's a dream of a setting. Not just drama either. Photoshoots, adverts, do up the kitchen and you could have weddings there if you apply for a licence. My sister runs a wedding consultancy. She's always on the look out for attractive countryside locations with civilised plumbing and good transport connections. I could put her in touch with you, if you like?'

'That would be great. Thanks, Coralie.'

'But Theo,' I said, bewildered. 'How

on earth would you ever have a say in what Wansdale Manor is used for?'

He met my eyes and reddened slightly. 'Ah. Well. Mostly because it's mine.'

9

'Bruce is worried,' said Coralie.

It was the next morning. I was standing by the shed, tying to remember what I'd been going to do this morning. I stared at her without understanding for a moment. I'd had the drive home, all night, the drive back this morning . . . and I was still knocked endways by the news that Theo Grainger, far from just being the heritage vegetable farmer from next door and general dogsbody, was actually the owner of Wansdale Manor. No wonder he was so keen on finding clues to the Wansdale Bounty. Not that he'd mentioned that. All he'd mumbled last night was that actually it was his dad who was the owner, he'd explain when he was less knackered, but meanwhile not to lose any sleep over having to find a new site for my plants. 'Did you know about Theo?' I asked Coralie.

'Yes, of course. He is the one we've been dealing with. Lady Mary was his great-great-great grandmother. He isn't the owner of the manor as such,' she added, scrupulously fair, 'but he's got the authority from his father to act for him. There is some sort of complicated family trust, I believe. Um, about Bruce . . . '

I gave up. I'd get no sense out of her while Bruce had a problem. 'Go on. Did you find out where he went yesterday evening, by the way?'

A shadow crossed her face. 'No, but I've still got a job this morning so I'm making the most of it. So anyway, he loves the footage of you fixing up Theo's leg and adored you pulverising those leaves and says it will make great TV, but it's the honey aspect. His trademark is accuracy, you see. If you could talk to him . . . '

'I'll do better than that. I'll show him the original reference.'

'Now?'

'Just as soon as I get to the terrace room and log on. Honestly, Coralie, I don't know why you are worried about being replaced. You're like a terrier where Bruce's itinerary is concerned. Nobody could be better at what you do.'

'Try telling my family that.'

I stopped dead. 'You're joking. You're brilliant. My family on the other hand . . . Let's just say that I bet you were never introduced in company as the person who'd grown the vegetables for lunch.'

Coralie pulled a face. 'Oh, that's harsh. Still, at least it's a positive. My people simply can't accept what a fantastic opportunity it is, career-wise, for me to be working with Bruce. All the comments I get are along the lines of how I'll never land a suitable husband unless I pretty myself up and find a more conventional occupation. Working for my sister Rosamund, for example, because she's being so brave and it would really help her out now

168

her husband's lost all their money and it's a little unfair to think of myself all the time and besides, it's a far more feminine way to pass the time before having children. Everyone knows weddings beget weddings.'

I snorted. 'So my family think I should be more intelligent, yours think you should pretend to be an airhead. What nonsense. Hey, wait a minute, weren't you defending Lady Mary a few days ago for just that same attitude?'

'Yes, but that was 1915 and this is now. That's my point. That's Bruce's whole theme in the documentary. We've moved on as a society, or we should have done. I don't see why I should be made to feel guilty just because Rosamund's tool of a husband invested in some shady scheme that anyone with half a brain could see was dodgy. I want to be good at something for *me*. I want someone to think I'm marvellous for what I am, not how I look. Can you talk to Bruce now, please?'

Bless the girl. She really did want it

all. 'I'm coming,' I said. 'You can trust me on one point, you don't need to prettify yourself up. You've already got exactly what it takes.'

'Thanks,' she said, clearly not believing a word of it. Mind you, when I caught sight of myself being efficiently chivvied past the French windows I could hardly blame her. Not many upmarket media types would take the word of a scruffy gardener held together by denim shorts, strappy top and a cotton headscarf.

In the terrace room I showed Bruce on the computer where I'd found Reverend Septimus Thomson's account of John Goode's visit to Wansdale, referring to the herb dial *and* to the monks' honey. He was thrilled with the reference, but still fretted that it wasn't mentioned anywhere in the house records as being specifically used in 1915.

'Are you sure?' I asked. Email alerts were suddenly pouring into my ear, distracting me. I concentrated on something that would convince him. 'It might have simply been too common to warrant a special note. Honey has been used — especially in the countryside — for centuries. I'd have said the first thing Louise would have done on seeing any weeping wounds would be to slather them with honey.' I was on shaky ground here. I knew it was what she *had* done (though the wintergreen had been my own idea), but I couldn't prove it without letting on I'd found her diary. I hadn't had a chance to look through the rest of the little desk yet, much less read the whole journal and I didn't want to pass anything over without knowing what else might be concealed.

There had to be some secret, otherwise why would the diary have been locked in the writing desk in the shed? Hadn't Theo said Louise had emigrated? Why hadn't she taken the desk with her? Thinking about it, the desk was rightfully Theo's if he owned the manor. Maybe I should give it to *him* rather than Bruce.

'What about the household accounts? Have you got those?' I asked. 'They'd show the usage of various items. I heard you mentioning to Mrs Merryweather that the housekeeper had complained to Lady Mary about foodstuffs being in short supply. Where did that information come from?'

Bruce quivered, as if scenting gold. 'Good thought! Lateral. I like that. We know Louise tends to Lt Wright's leg when they arrive, because Lady Mary points it out to Captain Percival Wright as an example of how selfless she is. There's nothing to say she might *not* have used honey on him. At the very least we could put it forward as a possibility. I'll check with Mrs Merryweather. She has the household accounts. She was very interested in them. Invaluable, of course, in her line of work.'

He hurried off. Coralie trotted behind him making notes as she went, leaving me alone in the research room.

I quickly logged into my email

account. This morning's flurry had been from Mum, detailing all the fields for sale in a ten-mile radius of home, suggesting that if I drove home tonight, we could whizz around them all tomorrow. I suppressed my instant reaction of total horror and replied to say thanks, but I'd found a site up here that was exactly right and I was going to be incredibly busy now until after I'd moved. I stayed in front of the computer, re-reading John Goode's passage about the herb dial that had first caught my eye. Then I went on to read the riddle. I heard a dragging footfall behind me. 'You haven't found it then?' I asked. 'The Wansdale Bounty?'

Theo put two steaming mugs on the table and pulled up a chair. 'It's a little difficult when the tenants won't let you on your own land.'

I eyed the tea. 'Is this a peace offering? Why didn't you tell me you owned the whole place?'

He grimaced. 'Dad and I have only just got Wansdale back. I'm still adjusting. And ... and there are complications.'

'What sort of complications? How long was it let for?'

'Seventy years in all. It's weird, having it back again, like being made whole but with a scary don't-blow-it-don't-blow-it-don't-blow-it thunder roll in the back of my head.'

'Ah, I know that feeling. Why would you blow it?'

'History, mostly. Have you read the script yet?'

'No, I've only got my cutaway scenes.'

'Ask Coralie for a copy. It's very close to the truth as I understand it. Basically, Louise's eldest brother died on the Somme, so Wansdale passed straight to the middle brother Edmund on the death of their father. Edmund and Geraldine and their children were already living here, along with Lady Mary. Louise married Lt Wright and they emigrated after the war. That's where the documentary finishes. What happened next was that during the *Second*

World War, Geraldine lost her husband and oldest son in that order. The order is important, because the double death duties were crippling and Geraldine's grandson was only a minor. Wansdale had already been requisitioned as a Forces hospital again, so she and Lady Mary, who was in her mid-70s by that time but still very much the matriarch, did a hushed-up deal with the tax office whereby the government took the manor on a long lease in lieu of cash. Lady Mary, Geraldine, Geraldine's daughter-in-law Pamela and her children all moved into the dower house.'

I stared at him, appalled. 'Three generations of women in one kitchen? Good grief.'

Theo grinned. 'That's roughly what Barbara says. She's my grandmother, but hates being called Gran because it makes her sound old. She was seven when they moved. Can you imagine it? Going from the freedom and space of the manor to all of them living on top of each other within sight of what they'd lost? It gave her an aversion to the place. She ran away with the local builder's son as soon as she could and moved into a nice modern bungalow in the village. Dad and Aunt Sue were brought up in as classless a fashion as she could manage, for which I'm not sure Aunt Sue has ever forgiven her.'

'Oh dear,' I said.

'Barbara was appalled when her brother died childless, because that meant the dower house passed through her, so to speak, to Dad. He had to wait until my great-grandmother died to move in, of course — you can't just eject elderly relatives, no matter how unpleasant they are — but he didn't mind the house one way or another, just thought it was handy that it came with enough land to start the vegetable business. Barbara says the only way you'll get her out of her bungalow is in a coffin.'

I chuckled. 'She sounds like my granny. Seventy-five years young and clinging obstinately to her 1960s semi because it's so much better than anything she grew up with. Mind you, the way she tells it, she spent her formative years in a prairie log cabin in a year-round blizzard, so maybe she's got a point. She thought she'd died and gone to heaven when she married an Englishmen and he brought her to London.'

'Tough generation, aren't they? Anyway, Wansdale stayed as a hospital for a while, then it became a research establishment. By that time the death duties had been paid off and the government didn't want the burden of the manor upkeep any more. They still held the lease though, so when this rich bloke took a liking to it they sold the lease on, but with the rent going into a family trust. This is where it gets complicated. The dower house belongs absolutely to my father and it will come to me. So does the manor. Strictly speaking, the lease money from the manor should have come down the male line too, but because Great-uncle David was only nine at the time, Lady Mary, Geraldine and Pamela had been the ones involved in setting up the deal. They wanted money to live on, so the trust is couched in such loose terms that virtually any member of the family who makes a fuss can claim a piece of the pie.'

'Messy,' I commented.

'Tell me about it. Any change of use of the manor to this day needs three family members to sign a release. Very fortunately, Bruce contacted us full of enthusiasm about using the manor before the previous lease was up, so I emailed the contract to Dad without telling anyone and he posted it back again. Barbara and I signed it afterwards. The rest of the family are furious with us for not renewing the lease. My aunt is particularly vociferous on the subject of her disappearing rent payments. There's also a set of removed cousins who are making restive noises and threatening to go over my head and appeal to the courts. None of them are entitled to the manor, none of them want to live in it themselves, nor do they have the faintest idea how much work would be involved renting it out on a regular basis. They're just greedy for returns. The possibility of the TV money is holding them at bay for the moment. It won't keep them off my back for much longer though, especially as my amateur read-through of the contract leads me to suspect they don't qualify for *anything* now the original lease has terminated. Aunt Sue has been bombarding me with texts and emails wanting to know when she can come over to the 'dear old place' to get acquainted with it. She's already planning an extended family Christmas here. I have a feeling good will to all men won't be on the agenda once she knows the full story.'

I studied at him as he scowled ferociously at the computer screen. 'Never mind them. How do *you* feel about the manor?' I asked.

He sighed. 'Proprietorial, I suppose. Stupid, isn't it? Wansdale has been next to me all my life. I can feel the separation of the two parts like a dull ache in my chest. More land memory, maybe. I'm not obsessed with grandeur like my aunt. I just want to make the manor work. For that I need investment and everyone else to take a step back.' He looked at me, part humorously. 'So, until we discover the Wansdale Bounty, how much can Wild About Herbs pay in rent?'

I told him what I paid the council. 'That includes a workshop and somewhere to live.'

He waved a hand. 'Plenty of spare rooms for a workshop. As for living, would the housekeeper's flat do you? The tenants spruced up a whole ground floor wing for the resident staff. I can take you along to see it now, if you like.'

'Are you kidding? Yes please.' I squinted sideways at him. 'I suppose this room is out of the question? I really love it. And do you get to keep all the herbals when Bruce has finished with them, because I'd like them as well. Otherwise I'll beg them off Coralie.'

'Is that a yes?'

'Of course it's a yes. How could you think otherwise? The situation is perfect, with or without warring relatives. I'll set Mum on them if you like. When can I start moving my plants?'

Bruce blew back in before Theo could answer. 'Found it,' he said briskly. 'Good hunch, Jen. Honey it shall be. Ah, I'm glad you're here, Theo. You two work well together. I want to get the factual massage scene in the can before the actors arrive. You don't mind if we use that scar on your thigh? Give it a touch of realism. Lavender cream, Jen. You'll need to make some. The stillroom is all set up now. Then you can talk through the properties as you rub it on. Coralie will find you a window this morning when Fran can film you mixing the lotion.'

My mouth dried. Rubbing cream on to Theo's scar would be quite different from dressing his gash as a holding measure. For a start, all the psychological blocks he'd built up over the years were still there, buried and twisted. I'd felt them briefly yesterday and had shied away, concentrating on the physical injury to the lower leg. It was all very well Bruce imagining I would simply be applying the lotion for the camera, but I knew perfectly well that as soon as my hands made contact with Theo's skin I wouldn't be able to ignore the old wound and its associated trauma. I started talking, fast. 'I was going to query that. The lavender element puzzles me. Lavender doesn't work that way.'

'But we have letters sent by various injured officers from the hospital here. One specifically states, 'Nurse Wansdale rubbed in her lavender cream again today. I am already able to walk a few steps and the pain is very much less.''

'And you used lavender on my neck,' Coralie put in.

'Lavender *oil*,' I corrected. 'It's used in aromatherapy to calm. I imagine Louise pounded flower spikes into a lot of her mixes to de-stress the patients. It would also have the advantage of disguising the smell of the carrying agent, which might be goose-grease or rendered animal fat.' The recipe, I thought with a stab of guilt, might be loose in the writing desk. I hadn't thought to look.

'What do you think she'd have used as the main ingredient if not lavender?' asked Bruce.

'English wintergreen, possibly,' *Ah, that was what I'd been meaning to look for. Louise had said there used to be some under the willow.* 'But that's quite scarce and would be saved for actual wounds. Most likely comfrey mixed with goose-grease in the early years of the conflict. Comfrey is an anti-inflammatory agent. It would aid joint mobility and help broken bones set more cleanly. It is called knitbone in the countryside.'

'Knitbone. Nice. Make some up, then. Add the lavender for accuracy. Then you can use it on Theo.'

Just like that. Okaaaay. Brace up, Jen. 'In that case I'd better pop back to my workshop now to fetch my big mortar and pestle and mixing bowls.' *Via Waitrose for goose grease,* I thought, but didn't trouble Bruce with that small detail. I wouldn't put it past him to demand that I buy a goose and render the fat down from first principles.

It was mid-afternoon by the time we got to the massage scene. Bruce was adamant that I use exactly the salve I'd prepared for the camera. Theo's nose wrinkled. 'I can see why the lavender,' he murmured.

I gave him a look. 'I thought you didn't have any shorts,' I said as he lay twisted away from me in a pair of cut-off denims on the replica hospital bed of the 1900s. He'd taken the dressing off his lower leg and had washed the wound. A quick inspection showed me it was healing fine.

'Correct. I didn't have shorts until roughly an hour ago. I was offered scissors or a genuine reproduction 1915 towel. As you'd already destroyed yesterday's jeans to the point of no repair, I finished the job.'

I suppressed a grin and dipped my fingers in the bowl of comfrey cream. From the first touch on the puckered skin of the scar, I realised he was as tense as I was. Man alive, this was going to be difficult. Eighty stitches, he'd said. It didn't bear thinking about. The trouble was, I couldn't shut it out. I added another couple of drops of lavender, whether for me or for him I wasn't prepared to say. I took a deep breath, made my fingers move, and started talking to the camera, explaining the technique and giving a bit of history. All the time I could feel buried in Theo's head the horror of the moment when he had fallen on to the railings. His body remembered it, his muscles shied away from me. I couldn't help it, I had to take that trauma away, I had to coat the memory in an analgesic, to start untwisting the psychological sinews as well as easing the physical ones. It wasn't in me to stop. Long after the camera had finished rolling and the crew had left, Theo still lay there.

'What the hell did you do?' he asked at last.

'What I always do. I tried to help. I couldn't not,' I replied. I lay back in the chair next to the bed, drained.

He rolled over to face me. 'I have never felt so exposed. You do know you've got a gift?'

I met his gaze shakily. 'I did tell you.'

'I don't know about you,' said Theo, 'but I need a large pot of tea. And cake. And I'd like it in my own kitchen, not surrounded by production crew. Can you walk?'

'Possibly.'

'Let's get out of here then.'

10

I followed Theo next door to the dower house, so tired I had trouble putting one foot in front of the other. 'I'll need to massage your leg again,' I said.

'Yeah, right. Maybe in a year or so,' he said. 'When I've recovered from today's assault.'

I watched as he cut two thick slices of bread and pushed butter and honey across the table to me. I knew I had to speak. 'I'm serious, Theo. I'm sorry if I hurt you, but the fall is still there in your head. You have to let go of it. Chris has taken lots of tumbles over the years — not as bad as yours — and he's always managed to shrug them off.'

'So have I before. The conventional wisdom among night walkers is that if you fall, you get up and do the route again. This time I was stuck in hospital for two months, so I couldn't.'

'What about when you came out? You must have had physio exercises to strengthen your muscles enough so you could walk. They wouldn't discharge you otherwise. You should have been given a programme to follow.'

He gave a mirthless smile. 'I was, but by the time I came out, the neighbours had smothered the boundary railings in high voltage electric wire. Mum and Dad were livid. They weren't best pleased with me either. Apparently it's not so very pleasant seeing your only son skewered along a length of railing. Mum can't even use the spiked joint dish to carve the Sunday roast any more any more.'

I was shocked into sitting bolt upright. 'The neighbours? It was here? You fell here? You were climbing the manor?'

Theo stared into the amber depths of the pot of honey. 'I was climbing the stable block. I thought I'd solved the Wansdale riddle. *Thyme on dial leads arrow straight* . . . I thought it must be

188

referring to the clock on top of the folly. You know, just as if no one else over the centuries had never thought of that before. I didn't know about the herb dial then. Don't forget, I only saw the manor garden for the first time on the same day you did.'

I groped for my tea, feeling sick.

'Don't look at me like that, Jen. I'd graduated with a First, I had a great job I was heading out to, I was fit in mind and body, plus I'd been using the roof-tops of Cambridge as a playground for the last four years. I was at the top of my game. I was good and I knew it. I studied the stable every which way I could, then went up it off the roof of the offices. Yes, it was technically trespass, according to the terms of the tenancy agreement, but it should have been a walk in the park. Except, *because* I'd studied the plans, I was concentrating on them instead of letting my feet find their own path. Coming around one of those blasted twisty corners, I fell. Straight on to the railings.'

My hand was clamped over my mouth to keep the screams in. 'And you've lived with those evil spikes bordering your garden ever since? Dear God, Theo.' No wonder the terror was still in his head. A permanent inflammation of the memory.

He nodded grimly. 'Trust me, as soon as the first payment arrives from the film company, they're scrap.'

I didn't honestly think I'd have left it that long. I said so. 'If it was me, they'd have been toast as soon as the rental period was over. Not one minute longer, whether I had the dosh to take them down or not.'

Theo's mouth twitched. 'I'm still hoping to implant the idea in Bruce's head that accurate *period* shots of the manor wouldn't show the railings at all.'

'You are shameless. Seriously, Theo, get them taken down. They aren't doing you any good there.'

'It's the money, Jen. Builders won't work for nothing. The vegetables only just pay for themselves as it is. And if the family start demanding their eighty percent of the documentary fees I'll need my twenty percent to contest them.'

I snapped my fingers. 'Family. That's it. My second brother Anthony is a lawyer.' I got out my phone. 'Have you got a copy of the trust agreement?'

'Such as it is. Yes. It's no good, Jen, I can't afford lawyers.'

'You won't have to if I phrase this the right way.' I texted Anthony, saying the words aloud as I tapped them in. *Hi, Anthony, I've found the ideal site for my business, but the owner can't rent it to me at a price I can afford unless he knows he has the right to without some archaic trust getting in the way. Can I email you the details? It's Chris's friend Theo Grainger from university. The living accommodation is in Wansdale Manor itself, no less!*

Theo looked at me with sardonic admiration. 'Not just a green-fingered healer, are you? Did you really just wrap up helpless-me, old school tie and snob-value in one text?'

I nodded modestly. 'Not bad, was it?'

'And you call me shameless.'

'My family irritate me beyond belief because they don't think I can fend for myself. I might as well use it for once. See? What did I tell you?' I added as my phone pinged back instantly. *Top news! Send me agreement and Theo's contact details.*

Theo stood up. 'No sooner said than done. Would you care to step into the office?' He paused. 'Jen, this is ridiculous. My head feels as if it's been invaded by Mordor's army, but I'm walking better already.'

I raised an eyebrow at him. 'That was the general idea.'

* * *

I can't really explain it, but once you've been inside a person's physical trauma, it's impossible to feel the same degree of detachment and wary reserve towards them. All through the next day, as I transferred my large tubs and containers across to Wansdale, I kept getting jabs of guilt about concealing Louise's desk from Theo. I vowed to myself that I would skim through the diary and look for lists of medical ingredients tonight before giving him the lot tomorrow.

Except, of course, that once I'd finished the tubs I was faced with a full order sheet and a reminder notice taped to the front door with a demand to arrange a date for leaving the premises. I took a photo of it in case I could sue the developers for harassment, then emailed an assurance that I was already moving my stock but it would take time. I packed up the orders and fell asleep at the kitchen table. By the time I woke it hardly seemed worth going to bed, so I just showered, changed and headed back to Wansdale to start digging nursery beds on the far side of the garden.

'You're keen,' commented Theo a couple of hours later. 'Are all your family this energetic? I've already had your brother Anthony on the phone twice. He was orgasmic over the trust agreement. Says it's promising to be the most fun he's had in years and he wouldn't dream of charging me for his time. How can a flaky-as-hell seventy-year-old agreement be fun?'

'Probably in the same way that clambering around deadly rooftops without a safety rope is fun. Lawyers are weird. I should warn you, by the way, that my family are all likely to visit as soon as I get settled. Far too good an opportunity for them to miss. Chris apparently waxed lyrical to them about the house this weekend. He did it to deflect Mum from his love life, but it's going to backfire on me. This is also pretty standard. Theo, there's something I have to tell you . . . '

But he was hurrying off. 'Later. I've got a restaurant order to crate up.'

Chris, predictably, turned up at lunchtime. 'Nice,' he said, looking around the garden as if assessing acreage.

'Hello, brother dear. Busy as usual, I see. I expect you'd like a coffee, would you? In the kitchen where the rest of the crew are likely to be?'

He grinned at me. 'Wouldn't say no.'

'Don't hurt her, Chris. She's surprisingly insecure under that efficient exterior. She's also by way of being a friend of mine.'

He tweaked my hair. 'I gathered.'

They had just finished filming Mrs Merryweather down the far end of the kitchen when we walked in. Bruce was in his normal huddle over the playback while Coralie hovered at his shoulder taking notes. She gave Chris a tiny wave. Chris fluttered his hand in reply.

Now that was new, I thought. Normally he'd have smiled knowingly.

'Something smells good,' he said.

One of the engineers waved at the table. 'Pound cake. Made with a pound of everything. Try it.'

We did. It tasted like a sweet, dense Madeira cake. I wrinkled my nose. 'Too sugary for me. Wasn't there a shortage during the Great War? I'd have thought they'd have to cut down on the ingredients.'

'That was World War Two,' said Chris.

I shook my head slowly. 'I'm sure it was the First World War as well. I did a project at school. Rationing was brought in towards the end.'

Coralie had been listening with half an ear. '1918,' she said. 'After our timeline. Mrs Merryweather did explain as she was cooking.'

'There would still have been shortages beforehand,' I said. 'I'd have thought she'd have to substitute grated carrots, or perhaps use some of Theo's honey. Or did Wansdale get extra supplies because of being a Forces hospital?'

Coralie's fingers flashed over her tablet as she made a note. 'Good thought. They might have done. I'll check. Oh . . . ' She broke off in agitation, seeing Chris wander down to the kitchen set.

'Sorry,' I said to her as we hurried after him. 'It's an occupational hazard,

I'm afraid. I forgot to warn him. Off the set, Chris. We're not allowed to touch.'

'Mrs Merryweather is very particular about hygiene,' added Coralie. 'Which is reasonable, considering the effort she's put in to source exactly the right heritage ingredients.' She dropped her voice. 'Expensive, though. I had no idea eggs *could* cost that much. I nearly died when I saw the pound cake ingredients set out on the table. It took ten eggs. *Ten*.'

I frowned. 'But . . . '

'I do apologise,' said Chris at his most charming. 'I was having a look at the oven. It's been niggling at me. I swear it's an American model.' He took out his phone and snapped a couple of shots.

'American?' squeaked Coralie, thoroughly dismayed. 'Oh no, it can't be. Mrs Merryweather specified it herself. What will Bruce say?'

Chris bathed her in his melting smile. 'I'm sure it will be fine,' he soothed. 'I daresay there was a catalogue where it could be ordered. The big American firms shipped all over the world. I'll find out for you.'

'Would you? That would be so amazingly nice. Thank you.'

Bruce was glancing across at us with a hint of impatience, presumably because Coralie had strayed out of note-taking range. 'What were you saying about the border railings, Chris?' I said, raising my voice as we moved back towards the cake. 'Period or anachronistic?'

'Completely wrong,' he said immediately. 'Faux Victorian. They look very impressive, of course. I daresay nobody except an architect would know.'

I turned my back on Bruce's outraged face. 'Or a historian, presumably?'

'Well, yes, naturally. Is Theo anywhere?'

'Coralie!' snapped Bruce behind me.

'He's next door, as far as I know,' I said, barely keeping my voice level. 'Shall I take you around?'

'Please.' He gave the crew a cheery wave and we made it outside before I was overtaken with a fit of the giggles.

Chris gave me an old-fashioned look. 'And that was about?'

I sobered instantly. 'Those bastard railings are what Theo fell on. He was climbing the stable block. The fall is still in his head, Chris. They need to be gone.'

I complain a lot about my family, but they have never once questioned me on the things that matter.

'Dear God,' muttered Chris, and on espying Theo checking off the contents of a vegetable crate against a printed order, called genially, 'Prepare for workmen some time soon. I just told Bruce the railings were faux Victorian.'

'Cheers, mate. That'll save a bob or two. Are you here to vet me as a landlord?'

'Amongst other things,' I said drily. 'Theo, I suppose Mrs Merryweather didn't collect eggs or honey or any sort of sweetening vegetable from you to make her 1915 cake, did she?'

'No. Why?'

'I'm getting a bit of an idea about her, that's all. How much are your most expensive eggs?'

'Jen, you don't need to buy my eggs. If you fancy an omelette, you only have to ask.'

'Well, thank you, but supposing I happened to accidentally entice Coralie down to the chicken run, how much would half a dozen eggs cost?'

He looked mystified. 'Price lists are in the office.'

'Perfect. Which are the fluffy-footed ones again?'

'The Brahmas. I suppose there is some point to this, is there?'

'Best not to ask, in my experience,' said Chris. 'Listen, Coralie mentioned you might be doing weddings next door once the documentary is over. If you want sympathetic restoration in those upstairs rooms, I'm your man. Mate's rates,' he added.

'That means don't even think of

asking anyone else,' I said.

Theo grinned at me. 'I worked that out.'

'I'll let you see Chris off the premises. I've got digging to do. I'd like to start moving plants as fast as possible if that's okay?'

'Whenever. The garden's all yours.'

I kissed Chris on the cheek and left them. The sooner my brother said his piece to Theo the better. It had always been completely useless not to expect any interference where my life was concerned. I put them both out of my mind and was getting on really well with the new beds when Coralie appeared, trailed by Fran.

'Go on?' I asked her.

She smiled apologetically. 'Headache tisane. Can we do it from gathering the herbs right to finished product?'

I dusted the soil off my hands. 'We can, but I find it more effective to use it dried, because . . .'

Coralie interrupted. 'Tell me as we gather it. I'm in such a rush. Some of the actors are coming down for costume shots tomorrow and I still need to sort out cars and travel.'

I raised my eyebrows. 'The tisane is for you, then?' Behind her, I noticed Fran had silently started filming.

Coralie brushed a hand across her forehead. 'Yes, normally I'd just swallow a couple of paracetamol, but . . . '

'Feverfew does act very much like a natural aspirin,' I said, collecting an enamel bowl from the shed. 'It's been used for centuries as a mild pain relief, due to its anti-inflammatory properties. Here you are, it's over here.'

Coralie wrinkled her nose at the scent as we reached the tall, grey-green stand with its tiny, branching daisy flowers.

I grinned. 'Sorry about that. It's another reason why dried leaves are better than fresh. I usually add lemongrass to calm it down a bit, but that wouldn't have been grown in this country in 1915.' I deftly cut a few long stalks and stripped the leaves off into a bowl. 'Interestingly, because feverfew contains Vitamins C and A and iron amongst other goodies, if you take it to alleviate period pains, it'll help to clear up any associated hormonal skin problems too.'

Coralie smiled wanly. 'Two for the price of one.'

'Something like. If we go up to the stillroom, I'll put this bowlful to dry and make you a cup from the dried leaves I prepared earlier.'

'Thank you.' She filled her lungs and tipped her face to the sun. 'It smells so healthy out here, doesn't it?'

'Yes, the Edwardians believed in fresh air and lots of soap. Good sanatorium practice. Excluding germs is all very well, but I do think modern medicine could benefit quite a bit from letting the outside world into the wards now and again. Tell you what, the tisane will take ten minutes to infuse, so we could carry it down to the beehives while it brews and add a bit of genuine Wansdale honey to sweeten it before you drink it. It's beautifully peaceful down there. I daresay lots of the injured officers found a measure of relief just sitting on the bank watching the river and contemplating nature.'

I had no expectation that this would work but, 'All right,' said Coralie, surprising me. 'If I'm testing the remedy, I ought to do it properly.'

Going past Theo a few minutes later, I gave the tiniest jerk of my head and directed a significant look at the egg boxes. Out of the corner of my eye, I saw him pick up a basket and follow us.

'I've organised the railings to come out,' said Coralie. 'That'll save time when we're filming. No more walking up one side and down the other like this.'

'It'll look accurate too,' I said. 'They wouldn't have been here in 1915 because it was all one property.' I had provided us with a clean teaspoon for Coralie's honey and stirred it in for her as we sat side by side on the bench. As I'd hoped, one or two of the hens came nosily across.

'Gorgeous, aren't they?' I said. I reached into the feed bin and scattered a handful of corn the way I'd seen Theo do. 'Don't you just adore the ones with the feathery feet? They're Brahmas, I think Theo said. Brought in from India in the mid-1850s.'

'I like the punks best,' said Coralie. 'I could just do a hairstyle like that.'

'Those are my Silkies,' said Theo, putting his egg basket down and making a complicated chittering sound as he crouched and stirred the corn around. More of the hens pattered across. He picked one up and brought it over. 'Stroke it, if you like. The feathers don't have retaining barbs like normal hens, which is why they look fluffy. Poor things get waterlogged when it rains, so I have to chivvy them into the hen house. They were introduced from China as early as the 1800s. Really good winter layers even when the other breeds have given up. Sometimes I think all they want to do is be mums.'

'The 1800s?' said Coralie slowly.

'Oh yes, most of today's modern hens are descended from the old breeds, but lots of producers still keep the pure rare-breed varieties. I've got Sussex Buffs over there. They were brought in by the Romans originally. My customers really like the eggs and I don't charge any more than the village shop.'

'Right,' said Coralie crisply. She drained the rest of her tisane in one purposeful swallow and stood up. 'Thank you, Jen. That was most effective. I feel all energised now.' She strode off.

'So,' said Fran, lingering behind, 'how are the light levels in this chicken shed of yours, Theo? I get the feeling the actors are going to be down here gathering eggs before many more pages of the script have passed.'

*   *   *

Towards the end of the day, Theo came to find me. 'I did mention my hens to Bruce at the same time as I told him about my vegetables,' he said.

'But presumably he didn't listen because Mrs Merryweather had already told him she had the protein sources organised. And she'd sussed that the more he pays for something, the more he values it and the less he questions its authenticity. I bet she was most put out to find there were already heritage vegetables and herbs on site.' I smiled at him serenely. 'Not that I suppose her to be getting commission on the foodstuffs or equipment *at all*.'

'For someone so young you are appallingly cynical.'

'Three older brothers,' I reminded him. 'And I'm not that young.'

He nodded at the pile of rubbish I'd cleared out of the beds. 'You want a hand putting that on the compost heap?'

'Yes please,' I said.

He hefted an armload. 'I owe you that omelette too. Coralie is updating my contract even as we speak.'

11

There were a couple of unfamiliar cars in the driveway when I arrived at Wansdale Manor next morning, but I paid them no attention. I was too busy unloading plants and trundling them down to my new bed. It had occurred to me that though Theo had said it was okay to start bringing in my stock, neither of us had let Bruce know. I hoped he hadn't had plans to do any filming where I'd been clearing yesterday but I was going to fill the beds without delay, just in case. After I'd emptied the van of my second load, I dodged into the kitchen to grab a thermos of tea and found Coralie making industrial strength coffee.

'Morning,' I said. 'Something wrong?'

'Bloody Louise suffers from hay fever,' snapped Coralie, tapping furiously on her tablet.

I immediately felt an immense,

inappropriate bubble of laughter well up. 'Oh no, she doesn't, does she?' I did my best to look sympathetic, but it wasn't easy. What a thing not to have checked. 'I'd forgotten you had some of the actors coming in. I take it you do mean the person playing Louise, not the real one?'

'Yes. Apparently she never lets it stand in her way and always doses herself up. Except today, when she read the script on the way here in the car and told the driver to make an unscheduled stop at the nearest chemist. She's sure she will be perfectly fine, but if we could be darlings and not do any outside costume shots until later . . . '

I had another sharp tussle with my facial expression. 'Yes, watery eyes and a runny nose might not be quite the look Bruce wants to promote. How on earth could she not know what the part entailed?'

'Actors,' said Coralie bitterly, 'are absolute masters at seeing what they want to see. I can understand her being so keen to work with Bruce that she overlooked the little detail of full health disclosure. Anyone would. What I don't understand is how she hadn't realised that the direction [Louise gathers basket of lavender] meant that she would actually have to gather a basket of lavender.'

'It does seem a little blinkered,' I agreed.

'And I'm the health and safety officer on this project so if she comes out in a disfiguring rash, ruining her chances of auditioning for whatever next year's Bafta-winning film is, it will be my fault.'

'If she's that bad, she'll carry an epipen,' I pointed out. 'Honestly, Coralie, if she didn't let you know when she signed the contract, I don't think you can be sued. Ask her to give you a full list of her allergies. Send me the script and I'll cross check the triggers with her scenes. As far as her hay fever today is concerned, I've got to go home for more of my plants anyway. I'll bring back some mint tea sachets and chamomile infusions. They should help with the symptoms.'

'You're an angel. Charge them to the budget.'

Well, naturally. I'd also put a stack of my Wild About Herbs business cards alongside them in the tea basket.

By the time the actors made an appearance in the garden after lunch, my new beds were looking innocently full and I was starting on the next level. At least for these, I didn't have to organise the plants with ease of filming in mind. I leant on my fork and watched with interest as a woman in a Red Cross nursing uniform and a 1915 soldier with a military-looking walking cane accompanied Bruce out on to the terrace. They did some shots in front of the house, then moved down the path, 'Louise' giving a small yelp as the slight breeze tugged at her starched head-dress.

Instantly, Coralie was by her side, attaching an invisible hairgrip. No one could have told from her professional demeanour how fluently she had been cursing the woman earlier. As they reached the herb dial, Bruce waved me across. The atmosphere, I realised, had changed. This was no longer the fringes of the project, making sure everything was accurate. This was the real thing.

'Louise, let me introduce Jen, our expert for the herbal remedies and massage cutaways. Jen, this is our Louise and our Lt Wright. You'll be seeing a lot of them out here when the filming starts.'

Louise reached for my hand and gave it a warm squeeze. 'Lovely to meet you,' she said in a beautifully modulated voice. 'I believe it's your chamomile tea I've been drinking all morning. Many thanks. I look forward to working with you.'

Lt Wright gave me a pleasant nod. It seemed strange not to know their real names but Coralie had already explained to me at some length that this was how Bruce preferred to work.

'I want a shot of Louise in front of

the herb dial, then we need to find a suitable place for the proposal scene. I was thinking down by the river, but seeing you both in situ, I believe a background of plants would be better.'

'The lavender bushes?' suggested Fran, lowering her camera. 'Near where we filmed Jen?'

Bruce tapped his teeth. 'Continuity, you think? Tying both sides of the documentary together? Yes, could work. Nice muted colours. Let's try it. You've learnt the scene, guys?'

The two actors immediately looked intelligent and helpful. 'Yes, of course,' they said in unison. 'Beautiful writing,' added Louise.

Behind everyone's back, Coralie rolled her eyes at me. I stifled another fit of the giggles.

They *were* professionals though. As soon as Bruce dropped his arm they became a shy, diffident Great War soldier and his nurse.

'I couldn't do this before,' said Lt Wright, gripping his cane and dropping very awkwardly to one knee, 'but now I can. Nurse Wansdale, Louise, will you do me the very great honour of accepting my hand and my heart.'

Louise gave a soft cry and bent to pull him to his feet. 'Oh, Archie, do get up, you ridiculous man. Have you really been waiting until you could kneel before proposing? Yes, of course I will marry you, and gladly. I hope I'll make you as happy as you have already made me.'

They embraced chastely and then turned to Bruce.

'Very nice,' he said, but he was looking pensive. 'Easier to do the proposal from a bench, I think. You can still look clumsy as you slide down on to one knee, but it will be more natural. Jen, where would you site a bench here?'

Me? I was pulled out of my startled thoughts. 'Um, next to the second lavender bush, I think, parallel to the house, not at an angle. I can extend the gravel along here to tie it in with the beds below. I've seen stone benches in gardens of this age, but I don't know where you'd get an authentic one from.'

'I'll put the props department on to it,' murmured Coralie, making a note.

They moved back up to the house, but I stayed where I was staring after them. *Archie*, she'd called him. Lieutenant Wright was Archie. So who had that sentence been about in the real Louise's diary? The one that ran *Oh Robbie, oh Robbie my love.*

★ ★ ★

'Jen, are you busy?' Theo appeared from around the shed. The removal of the railings had made quite a difference to the working of the garden. It felt very much more cohesive now. It also made it easier for people to sneak up on me. 'Jen? Oh, there you are, have you got half an hour?'

I had, but I'd been going to sit down with a bottle of water and read Louise's diary. I was absolutely shattered with all the digging, moving and planting I'd done so far today. I sighed. 'Yes, do they want me again? I thought the actors had gone.'

'They have, and Bruce is busy, which means Coralie is temporarily free to be a witness. It won't take long. I just want to whizz over to Barbara's bungalow to sign your rental agreement. We'll only have only two family signatures, not three, but I can email it to Dad to add his name when he next touches base somewhere with WiFi. It should hold Aunt Sue at bay for a little while.'

I shut the shed. *Sorry, diary, another time.* 'Okay. Why do we need to do it immediately?'

'Because my dear aunt has just texted to say she's coming over next week. I've told her not to as the filming will be in full swing, but she'll take no notice. She's a great one for firing off texts, not so hot at reading anything people send to her.'

We arrived at the front of the house to find Coralie waiting. 'I can't be long,' she warned.

'Shall I drive?' I fished out my keys

and I saw her recoil at the prospect of getting into the van. 'It's better than it looks,' I said.

'Definitely cleaner than mine,' added Theo.

A 4×4 drew up next to it. 'Or I could take us,' said Chris. 'Where are we going?'

'How very timely,' I said. 'We're off to Theo's grandma in the village to sign my lease. What are you doing here? Much more of this and you'll give working architects a bad name.'

'Do I need a reason to visit my sister?'

'You've never not had one yet.'

'I'm waiting on approval for the plans before I can get on and I wanted a look at the manor again. I've been having sympathetic restoration thoughts.' His eyes slid sideways to mine. 'Plus, Mum might possibly want photos of the housekeeper's flat if I happened to be thinking of helping you move in.'

Families. I huffed crossly. 'And this is you being discreet, I suppose.'

Coralie gave my hand a sympathetic squeeze. I was so surprised I forgot my bad temper and anything else I'd been going to say.

Theo was already opening the passenger door. 'We'll get to it after this, if you don't mind? You can witness the agreement too. An extra signature should give my aunt even more pause for thought.'

'No problem,' said Chris. He eyed Theo's boots. 'You wouldn't like to get in the back with Jen, I suppose? I do occasionally drive clients in this car.'

And this way Coralie sat next to him.

Theo's grandma was lovely. 'I'll sign anything you like, providing I don't have to move back there,' she said. 'As soon as George and I closed this front door against the world, I felt myself relax for the first time in nineteen years. I'm sorry Sue is making trouble for you, Theo. She always did have a streak of entitlement to her. I put it down to her spending all that time at the dower house with my mother and grandmother when your father was so ill as a child and I had to be with him in the hospital. Mother wasn't so bad, but Geraldine Wansdale was a bitter woman and I daresay her attitude rubbed off on Sue.'

'I wanted to ask you,' I said as I signed the agreement and then the others put their names to it. 'Was there a gardener at the manor when you were small?'

'A gardener? Oh yes. Mr McGower. A Scot in exile. Scared me to death. He carried on looking after the grounds until the government sold the lease. Then he tyrannised everyone in the village for the next few years by hiring himself out as a jobbing gardener. He had one of the original estate cottages that went with Wansdale. When we moved out, Great-grandmother decreed those dwellings should go to their inhabitants as a reward for long service.'

'That was a nice gesture.'

Barbara chuckled. 'From what I gathered afterwards, they all needed repairs and the government didn't want to take them on anyway.'

I grinned. 'It was still nice of her. Was that Lady Mary? She's going to be in the documentary.'

'So Theo tells me. She'd have hated that. Gross impertinence, she'd have called it.'

Coralie had been growing politely restive, but her attention was caught by this. 'Oh, of course. You actually knew her. Oh, gosh, we should have talked to you before. I can't believe we've missed the potential of such a primary source. What was she like?'

'Very imperious, dear. She was the lady of the manor until the day she died. George used to say her back was so straight you could hang wallpaper by it. David and I were terrified of her.'

'I don't suppose you knew Louise, did you?' I asked.

'Great-aunt Louise, would that be? No, she emigrated twenty years before I was born. She used to send letters two or three times a year with news of her family and the life out there, but when Great-grandmother died, the families lost touch. I daresay it was Geraldine's doing.'

'Coralie needs to get back, so we'd better fly,' said Theo. He bent and kissed Barbara's cheek. 'Thanks for signing. I'll come over and see you properly during the week. You know where I am if you need me.'

'That I do.' She turned a bright eye on me. 'Come over too, dear, if you want to hear more about the manor. Bye David. Nice to meet you.'

Theo smiled. 'Not David. Jen's brother is Chris.'

'Silly me. Of course he is. I'm old, you know. I get confused.'

I couldn't help it. I laughed out loud. 'You sound just like our granny. She pretends she's old when it suits her, doesn't she, Chris? I'd love to come again. Thank you.'

Coralie's phone pinged twice in the short time it took to get back to the manor. Bruce was pacing the Great

Hall waiting for her.

'Where have you been?' he asked accusingly.

'Witnessing Jen's rental agreement for Theo. I told you. I've also been talking to his grandmother about Lady Mary. Bruce, she *knew* her. She was very young when they all moved out and Lady Mary was over seventy, but apparently Lady Mary was totally Grand Dame right to the end of her life. Oh, and she always held herself absolutely upright, posture-wise.'

Bruce stared into the distance. 'Did she now? That's useful. Yes, yes, I can see her. Very good. Add it to the character notes.'

Coralie glanced at her tablet. 'Also, Barbara didn't know Louise, but she said her own grandmother, Geraldine, wasn't always very pleasant.'

Theo and Chris had turned away. I started to leave too. I was stopped by the sound of my own name.

'Authenticity. Good. Add that too,' said Bruce. 'Now then, do Jen and Theo know which vegetables and herbs to provide for Mrs Merryweather on Thursday?'

Coralie frowned, tapping her screen. 'She's not here on Thursday. She's here Friday. You've got the historical prosthetics man coming over on Thursday for his cutaway.'

'We'll have to do cooking as well. Mrs Merryweather asked if we could bring it forward. She has a medieval banquet at the weekend that she needs extra time to prepare for.'

'Right,' said Coralie, an edge to her voice. 'I'll rearrange the schedules to fit in both her and the prosthetics expert. What is she making? She hasn't sent a list.'

'Pork, I believe. Ping her and ask. Really, Coralie, I can't do everything.' Bruce strode off. 'Fran, let's run through today's footage. Notes, Coralie, please.'

'Tell me again what she sees in him?' murmured my brother.

'Energy,' I murmured back. 'Vision.

A sense of something marvellous coming together.'

'If you say so. Going to give her another massage later?'

'I'll certainly offer one. Run away and play with Theo. I've got more flower-beds to clear. The developers are offering me a two hundred quid incentive to be out by the end of next week.'

12

I prepared more ground, I moved plants, I prepared more ground again. I went home, filled orders, ate distractedly, fell into bed and repeated the pattern next day. I answered a congratulatory text from Mum on the size of the housekeeper's flat, gave Coralie a massage and she remembered she was supposed to be emailing me a copy of the script and Louise's allergies.

'Your brother,' she said in an offhand voice as she tapped away on her tablet. 'Is he . . . seeing anyone?'

'Not as far as I know,' I said carefully. 'I'm very fond of Chris, but he isn't good at commitment and I don't know why.'

She nodded. 'Okay. Thanks.'

It wasn't until later, over yet another hasty toasted cheese sandwich for supper, that I had time to check Louise's herbal scenes. There was nothing allergy-wise for her to worry about to begin with. The script opened before the war with Louise Wansdale being poshed up for an evening party by her maid, her mother looking on critically. As I'd read in Lady Mary Wansdale's letter, Louise was a plain girl who knew her own mind. The evening did not go well. Then there were a couple of scenes with her digging and weeding in the garden, then the family eating a meal when the news of the outbreak of war arrived. One of the village boys signed up and was killed almost at once. Louise pleaded to become a Queen Alexandra nurse, but her mother refused. The menfolk were shown going off to war, then came the news that Wansdale Manor was to be an auxiliary rehabilitation hospital. Louise, who had been quietly doing more and more work in the herb garden, said she could combine gardening with VAD Red Cross nursing. This time, Lady Mary agreed.

I skipped over the scenes where Lady Mary clashed with the new matron of the hospital and dealt with the cook's problems catering for mass eating on a diminished budget. The bits where Louise was pushed by her mother towards the eligible Captain Percival Wright all took place indoors, so they were okay. The gradual process of getting to know his younger brother, Archie, on the other hand, was spent increasingly outside as he worked on his mobility. The scenes showed him helping with the hens and the honey, spreading herbs to dry, enjoying physical tasks. It culminated in the proposal scene in the garden.

I switched my computer off when I'd finished reading, vaguely dissatisfied. I suppose it was reasonable that the documentary was slanted towards Lady Mary and her struggle to accept a more classless society. The social change was what Bruce was focusing on. Louise's part in it was a sub-plot illustrating the way Lady Mary couldn't even control her own daughter in these unsettled times. But . . . but reading the first few pages of Louise's diary, I knew she was more interesting than Bruce had written her. *He* didn't know that, though, because he hadn't had access to enough primary material about her. All he had was Lady Mary's point of view, and grateful commendations on Louise's nursing from the wounded soldiers.

I wanted to know more. I wanted to know about Robbie, whoever he was. I wanted to know why Louise and Archie had emigrated. I promised myself that tomorrow I would read the rest of Louise's journal. Then I'd better let Theo know about it, and after that — depending on what we found — we could decide what to tell Bruce.

As I rolled into bed, I wondered if Louise had continued to keep a diary after she emigrated. Anyone who wrote dutifully to her family two or three times a year would be quite likely to record her struggles with a new world. As soon as I'd moved into the manor and was properly settled, I'd look her up.

* * *

'I've emailed you the trigger scenes,' I said to Coralie, 'and suggested which parts of the garden it might be better to avoid. Does Bruce always work this way? He seems to be putting more emphasis on the historical accuracy than on the story.'

Coralie fired up defensively. 'It's what he does. Accuracy. What do you mean?'

'Nothing really, just that the storyline itself felt a little flat. Probably just me not fully appreciating the documentary style. How did everyone get on afterwards?'

'After what?'

'After the end of the script.'

She looked blank. 'Why would we know that? The focus is on the social change during the Great War. Anything beyond that is out of the timescale. Lady Mary and Geraldine stayed here until they moved to the dower house after the Second World War. Louise and Archie emigrated a few years after this war. That's it.'

And that, I reflected cynically, was why Bruce would always be chasing investments for documentaries. If he went at it with more of a *Downton Abbey* outlook — following the ups and downs of the families — he'd have audiences and contracts to burn.

'Is there anything special you want me for today?' I asked. 'Otherwise I'll carry on shifting plants.'

'Just the herbs for Mrs Merryweather. I still don't know which.'

'If it's pork it will probably be sage. I've got everything she asked for originally; it's the quantities I don't know.'

'Right. Oh — ' Her tablet chirruped at her. 'There you are. She would like sage and mint too, please. Apparently pork chops wrapped in minted breadcrumbs were a thing. I've never heard of the combination. Have you?'

'No, but she's the expert.'

'She'd have to be, for her money.' Coralie sighed as she read further. 'And she wants the whole kitchen cleared of crew and scrubbed down before the meat arrives mid-morning.'

'She's couriering the meat in?'

Coralie glanced at me with guilty eyes. 'I know. I've had words with Bruce about that. I do hope I haven't offended him, but honestly, her ingredients are frightfully expensive and come from bespoke suppliers, and I don't quite see how cooking for the camera would look any different if she used pork chops from the supermarket, do you?'

'No different at all, I'd say. It would be another matter if you were putting on a full WW1 Experience day like the Living History people. Then you could charge for the authentic taste of home-grown, home-cured pot roast, or whatever.'

'That's exactly what I said!' Coralie looked relieved that someone understood. 'Oh, that's something else Theo could do to drum up cash for Wansdale, isn't it? I wonder if he'd like to buy the set dressing furniture off us? It would save me disposing of it. It's all so difficult. I agree entirely with Bruce that the historical methods of cooking should be explained, but how can the taste matter? That level of detail is simply inappropriate in this case. As things are, Mrs M's materials are taking up a significant chunk of the budget. Sponsors don't exactly grow on trees.'

Poor Coralie. She really did have the cares of civilisation on her shoulders. I wondered if it was time to introduce a fragment of the real world. 'Have you considered asking her to find a cheaper supplier?' I said. 'It might work, although she won't like the reduction in her commission, I don't suppose. Or you could sweeten the pill by inviting the sponsors here to dine on the fruits of their investment. It would be a bit of a blow to the crew, mind. They look forward to cooking days.'

I could almost see the cogs meshing into place in Coralie's head. 'They'll have the catering vans from next week,' she said distractedly. 'Oh, Jen, how stupid of me. I never gave commission a thought. I *knew* eggs couldn't possibly be that expensive. Do you really think she's on the take?'

'Why else would she mislead you as to the difficulty of supply? Theo says lots of suppliers sell eggs from rare-breed hens. She'll know that, but she'd have no reason for thinking Bruce would.'

'Of course he wouldn't. He's dedicated to the programme.' She looked at me, appalled. 'It's such a betrayal of trust. I should have suspected though.'

I gave her a hug. 'Why would you? You've got a lot on your mind. See you later. I'll get on with preparing the next bed. I swear my muscles are growing muscles. I don't mind really. I am just so grateful to Theo for offering me the space.'

'Tricky, though, with him being your landlord now.'

I felt a prickle of unease. 'In what way?'

Coralie fidgeted, faintly awkward. 'Oh, well I just thought . . . you seemed to be getting on quite well, that's all. It's difficult having a relationship when business intervenes. I did it once. Never again.'

A relationship? With Theo? I felt myself come out in heat bumps. 'We're just colleagues, that's all,' I said. 'And friends.'

As I dug and cleared old bedding, what Coralie had said niggled at me. Theo and I *were* just friends and colleagues. I hadn't had a boyfriend since . . . well, since forever. I'd discovered very early that holding hands with a boy made me aware of his churned up feelings. The glut of raw emotion shocked me rigid when I was an inexperienced teenager. Physical breaks and injuries I could cope with. Hot mental tangles were messy and overwhelming and very scary. I had to shut them out before they affected me. Which meant I then grew cold towards whichever poor lad fancied me and he backed off in confusion. I'd got better at screening things out as I'd got older, and had managed a couple of noncommittal relationships at university, but it was horribly disconcerting to kiss someone and feel vast surges of adrenalin pumping at you. I didn't want to spoil my friendship with Theo by knowing about all his sexual urges milling around in the background. And yet, a relationship without passion was a dreadfully bleak prospect, as flat and unemotional as Bruce's script. I didn't know what the answer was. For now, I'd take being busy and single and preferably not hurting anyone in the process.

* * *

Yesterday's pleasant breeze had evaporated. It was another sticky, warm day. The sort of weather when it was inevitable I should get a text to say the gravel I'd ordered was on the delivery truck's next stop. My body felt like lying down and drumming its heels in protest. I'd been working non-stop transferring plants. Now I was going to have to shovel a couple of tonnes of stones too. My conscience kicked in, reminding me it was what I was being paid for. *Brace up, Jen.*

I'd emptied one tonne bag and was part way down the next when a very, very shiny Range Rover drove up to the house.

A woman, so dazzlingly smart that it hurt to look at her, swivelled out of the driving seat in the way I'd never got the hang of and pushed her sunglasses up to her forehead. An older woman, similarly smart, stepped leisurely out of the passenger side. Both of them looked at the manor in appraisal.

'Does one just knock?' I heard the younger woman murmur.

I transferred another shovelful of gravel from the tonne bag to my barrow. Who were these people? Surely not Theo's relatives? They'd have known to go next door.

The older woman beckoned to me. 'Excuse me,' she said, loudly and slowly. 'I'm looking for the lord of the manor.'

It was reprehensible of me, I know

it was reprehensible of me, and after all, I *was* wearing grubby shorts and a strappy top with green plant streaks across it. It was understandable that a cut-glass Englishwoman might think I was the migrant help, but even so . . .

'It's veg box day,' I said helpfully. 'He'll be next door.'

The woman took a deep breath. 'We. Wish. To. See. The. Owner.'

I opened my mouth to repeat that it was veg box day, when we were interrupted (probably fortuitously) by Chris driving up with a stone bench in a dinky trailer attached to the back of his car.

'Hi, Jen. I've got Bruce's bench. Do you know where he wants it?'

He swung down and began untying the rope tethers.

'Since when are you the props department?' I asked.

To my amazement, he blushed. Actually blushed. 'Coralie asked if I knew of an authentic one locally.'

The two women advanced on Chris, hands outstretched.

'Hello, I'm Rosamund Deverell,' said the younger one. 'We've been emailing.'

'So nice to meet you at last. Such a gorgeous house. The photos don't do it justice,' said the other.

Rosamund? I turned away to swallow a hysterical laugh. *Theo*, I texted, *you need to be here. This is just so funny.*

There was a clatter from the doorway. 'Was that a van, Jen? Mrs M's delivery still hasn't . . . oh my God,' shrieked Coralie. 'Mother! Rosamund! What are you doing here?'

'Coralie dear, there's no need to sound so surprised. Rosamund has been corresponding with Theo ever since you mentioned the possibility of Wansdale Manor as a wedding venue, so as we were passing . . . '

'This is Shropshire. The only way you would be 'just passing' from St John's Wood is if you had been suddenly taken with an urge to visit North Wales.'

Unnoticed, Theo cut across the front of the stable block. 'What is it, Jen? I'm only half-way through the veg boxes,

238

what with having to string up a double length of onions for Mrs Merryweather at short notice.'

He was in truly disgraceful cargo trousers today, with a faded T-shirt even more mud streaked than mine. Perfect. 'Unexpected guests. Coralie's mother and sister,' I whispered. 'Did you know they were coming?'

He shot a horrified glance at them. 'No, I damn well didn't. Even if I had, I wouldn't have made an appointment on veg box day. Ah hell, and I could do with Rosamund's custom too. I wonder if I've got time to change?'

'Not a chance. Watch this. They think Chris is you.'

'Rosamund has an A-list client in the area, dear,' replied Mrs Deverell, still smiling, 'and I do think it was the teeniest bit naughty of you not to mention how really very handsome Mr Grainger is.'

Coralie's fists clenched, her expression a mixture of impotence, fury and shame. Chris crossed the ground in two strides and put a casual arm around her shoulders. 'You reckon? Ugly so and so, I always think.' He dropped a kiss on Coralie's forehead. 'I've brought your bench, love. Have you got someone who can give me a hand shifting it? Jen will show me where.'

'Yes, of course,' said Coralie in a brittle voice. She whisked out of his arm and rattled indoors, reappearing with a couple of the crew.

'Oh, but . . . ' said Rosamund.

'Cheers,' replied Chris. He nodded pleasantly to Coralie's mother and sister. 'Nice to meet you. Where are we going with this, Jen?'

'Follow me.' As I picked up the barrow handles to wheel the gravel around to the lavender bushes, Theo strolled forward.

'Hi,' he said, holding out an only slightly earthy hand for Coralie's sister to shake. 'I'm Theo Grainger. Did you want to look at the principal rooms? I can't give you very long, I'm afraid, because it's my day for making up the vegetable boxes, and besides, there's filming going on. I'm afraid the manor is rather in demand at the moment. You'll get a quick impression, though of course the furniture is set up for the documentary.'

'You can't go anywhere Bruce is filming,' said Coralie sharply. 'He's got the prosthetics expert in the small sitting room, Theo. Mrs M is still setting up in the kitchen. Her delivery is very late.'

'But . . . ' Mrs Deverell was clearly bewildered. 'Then who is . . . ?'

Theo followed her gaze to where Chris, in crisp Chinos and a faultlessly pressed short sleeved shirt, was helping to lift the bench off the trailer. 'Chris? Oh, he's my architect. Nice chap. Knew him at Cambridge. Now, in here and have a quick look at the Great Hall. This is where I envision the receiving line for your wedding guests would be . . . '

We had sited the bench (which looked absolutely right, well done, Chris) and finished spreading the gravel by the time Theo brought Coralie's mother and sister out to the terrace. To her credit, Rosamund was ignoring her mother and making notes on her iPad every bit as efficiently as Coralie. Watching at a distance I could see the family resemblance.

'Harridan,' murmured Chris. 'Still, into every life a little rain must fall. I'll cope.' He started up towards them.

'Chris, are you serious?' I said, catching his arm.

He looked at me with a half-reluctant smile. 'I think I am. She's gorgeous and clever and focused and doesn't want anything from me except to be myself. Don't tell them at home yet. I need to give Coralie time to consider the idea of a relationship.'

My mouth may have fallen open as I pushed my wheelbarrow up the path after him. For the first time ever, my brother wasn't using his charm to get the girl he wanted. I was just about to whisper him luck when we were interrupted by a man in a white tradesman's coat striding belligerently around the side of the house.

'Where d'you want this pig, guvnor?' he said to Theo in accents that were pure North London. 'I've got to drop it and run. Helluva time getting here. Bloody satnav had you on the other side of the M6.'

'I . . . pig?' repeated Theo blankly.

'Yeah, pig. As ordered. Organic Gloucester Old Spot, home fed and bred. It's in the van.'

Theo's eyes met mine across the terrace balustrade. 'Kitchen?'

I shrugged. 'I guess. No wonder Mrs M needed all those onions. I'm just wondering how many sage bushes I've got with me.'

Theo gave a snort of laughter. 'Bring it around here,' he told the van driver. 'I'll hold the door open for you.'

The man reappeared with the goriest pig carcase I have ever seen. I didn't blame Coralie's mother for giving a faint scream when she saw it. It was, however, nothing to the shriek of rage

Coralie emitted as she shot out of the kitchen door a moment later.

'Come back here and take this away this instant,' she yelled. 'This was *not* what I okayed for the budget. A nice hand of pork chops was what I was told.'

'And that's just what you've got, darlin'. That and the rest. You just have to separate 'em out.' There was a malodorous roar as the van disappeared.

Coralie whirled around. 'This is ridiculous. Mrs M will have to speak to her supplier. I am not paying for an entire carcass when all we ordered was . . . '

'We did,' said Bruce. He had also come out of the kitchen door and was standing, half-impatient, shooting wary glances back inside.

'Pardon?' said Coralie.

'We did order the whole carcass. Don't forget, people were having problems with meat shortages. Many households during the war years kept a pig for fattening. Mrs Merryweather had the marvellous idea of showing how the entire animal would have been used with no wastage.'

Coralie looked at her tablet. 'When?' she asked, scrolling down her screen. 'When did she have this idea? I don't have a record of it. No notes, no emails, no estimates of how long the preparation and filming will take.'

'It was last week when she gave me dinner at her house. Didn't I mention it? Fabulous brawn pate. Splendid slow-cooked belly pork with cabbage. A symphony of careful cutting and cooking. Mesmerising in its way. It really shows what can be done, even in adverse circumstances.'

'Right,' said Coralie in the voice of someone who is striving very hard to be reasonable. 'So how long is this new segment going to take? I'll need to add it into the schedule.'

The cook herself appeared at the kitchen door, imperturbable and clearly considering herself free from blame. 'I'd have started on the preparation already if the driver had been here on time. *If there* are no more interruptions, I'll get a good deal done today and finish off the rest after the weekend.'

That was the moment Coralie snapped. Her voice rose. 'After the weekend? We are going to have that pork on the premises until next week? I don't believe this.' She turned to the terrace, her fingers already busy on her tablet. 'Theo, nearest butcher?'

'Dewsbury in the village. Traditional meats and cuts a specialty.'

'Here, what are you up to? I'm not using just anyone's meat,' said Mrs Merryweather, bristling. 'My suppliers are top class and authentic. I'm warning you, Bruce. This won't do at all.'

'I'm not buying more meat,' said Coralie through gritted teeth. 'I doubt we'll be able to afford so much as a sausage roll after you've robbed us blind for a whole pig. God, your commission must be astronomical. What I need to do is rent storage space in Mr Dewsbury's cold room for the carcass. We've got a full set of actors and ground crew arriving next week and it's ninety degrees in the bloody shade. Have you any idea what will happen to our schedule — not to mention our insurance premiums — if they all go down with raging salmonella? Bruce, I know this is your project and I believe in you one hundred percent, but I really must insist on full disclosure. I can't do my job unless you tell me exactly what it is you've been conned into as a result of becoming a devotee of Real Food.'

'Conned?' Mrs Merryweather's considerable bosom expanded. 'I have never in my life been so insulted.'

'The prices you charge, I imagine your clients are too afraid to. Emperor's New Clothes syndrome, I believe it's called. Oh, and another thing I've been meaning to mention. That ludicrously expensive cooker you insisted on is American.'

'How dare you!'

'American?' squawked Bruce, paling much as Coralie herself had a few days ago.

Coralie nodded. 'Fortunately, Chris

has managed to track down a catalogue showing a similar oven which could have been bought and imported if Lady Mary's husband had the right connections.' She looked back at her tablet. 'Dewsbury. Found him. I'll book that cold storage. Will he come and collect, Theo? I can't think either your van or Jen's will be suitable for transport.'

'I expect so,' said Theo.

'Good.' Coralie's gaze travelled to where her mother and sister were staring at her in stupefaction. 'Have you seen everything you need, Rosamund? We are rather busy here, as it happens. Another time it might be better if you emailed Theo in advance to make an appointment.'

She didn't wait for an answer, just put a hand to her earpiece and walked to the edge of the terrace, looking across the garden beds, every line of her a woman in total charge. 'Mr Dewsbury? My name is Coralie Deverell, I'm working at Wansdale Manor. I'm so sorry to bother you, but I have a problem that

I'm hoping you'll be able to help me solve . . . '

Coralie's mother and sister pulled themselves together. 'Well, it's been most instructive,' said Rosamund to Theo. 'I'll be in touch. Come along, Mother, or we'll have to pay Brigitta an extra hour's money for looking after the children.'

'An *American* stove, Martha?' said Bruce in tones of deep disappointment as he and Mrs Merryweather withdrew into the kitchen.

Theo's phone rang. 'Oh, God, the veg boxes,' he said, thumbing the busy button. 'You couldn't give me a hand, I suppose, Jen? I'm usually on my rounds by now. I'll help you cart plants later to make up for it.'

I cast a swift glance at Coralie, still talking on the phone. Chris made the tiniest shooing away motion with his fingers. 'Sure,' I said. 'Lead me to it.'

As we headed next door, I heard Coralie finish her phone call and Chris move across the terrace to say, 'Coralie, you were magnificent . . . '

13

It was very soothing picking runner beans in the orderly quiet of Theo's market garden. The cool green corridors between the tall rows were a welcome change from the Mediterranean heat of my herb beds. 'When do I stop?' I called across to him.

'When you run out of decent size beans. I've trained my customers not to expect any particular weight. I just divide what I've got between the boxes until they look full. Anything left over, I eat myself or freeze.'

'And the clients pay by the week, so you've got a regular income? That's useful. Have you always done them?'

'The veg boxes were my idea as a thank you to Dad. When I came out of hospital I found it was therapeutic helping him with the market garden. Then Mum was made redundant, so as

I was handily not showing any signs of rejoining society, they decided to treat themselves to a round the world trip, leaving me to look after everything.'

'When are they due back?'

'How long's a piece of string? They've been gone three years so far.'

My eyes widened. 'Must have been a hell of a redundancy package.'

'They find bits and pieces of work along the way. I needed the space, Jen. They knew it. Thing is, now I want to do more. Chris was right, I ought to be using my brains again. I want to make a success of the manor and I've got a few ideas, but I want to do it for me and Dad, not the rest of my freeloading family.'

'Hopefully Anthony will be able to untangle that agreement for you.'

'With any luck.' There was a pause as we worked our way down our respective rows, then he spoke again, his voice muffled. 'It's weird. Since you massaged my leg, I've felt more in control of my life. How is that possible?'

Ah. This was going to be awkward. 'Are you sure it's not the sudden influx of TV people into your solitary world acting as a wake-up call?'

I could see between the plants to where he stood. His back was rigid. He shook his head. 'I don't think so, although they do bring home what a recluse I've become.'

Deep breath time. 'When I was rubbing the cream into your leg, I could feel a constant chafing in your muscles. You're not going to like this, but it was almost as if you'd decided you didn't deserve to get better and you were hanging on to the pain to prove it. I suppose what I did was to apply a mental analgesic, then nudged your body into starting the repair. I'm guessing the new outlook is a knock-on effect. With one part of you suddenly working again, your head no longer needs to keep hold of its padded bandage.'

Complete silence, whether of shock or anger I couldn't tell. We finished picking the runners and took the trugs through to Theo's barn to divide the beans between the boxes. I loved the barn. Ordered seasons of growth and harvest and storage hung in the air, just as they did in my shed. It breathed a hundred years of quiet, purposeful work.

'I'd never failed at anything before,' Theo said at last. 'I'd always succeeded at anything I put my mind to. Is that it, do you think? A sort of inverted denial? I couldn't recover because that would mean admitting there was something to recover from?'

'Maybe. It could equally have been profound shock to begin with, which is only now wearing off. I'm not a psychologist. I just know that the trauma is still there inside you and it won't leave until you let it. Do you want me to have another go at your leg later?'

'No. Yes.' He stared at the open doorway, his hands tangled in runner beans, and took a ragged breath. 'I don't know, Jen. Yes, I think. It's time. Do you mind?'

'I wouldn't have offered otherwise.'

★ ★ ★

Theo was as good as his word and followed me home in his van once we'd delivered his orders. St Martin's was already a dispirited wasteland of drooping red-hatched tape and safety boarding. My part was the only cheerful section. A small green oasis.

'I need to set up a change of address with the post office,' I said, picking up the mail. 'Does the housekeeper's flat have its own letter box?'

'If not, I can easily put one in,' said Theo. 'The sooner the better. Tomorrow, if you like. Jen, this is horrible. I don't like to think of you here alone at night. The site is an invitation to thieves. Good Lord,' he added, coming in after me and staring at my crowded living room.

'It was the school caretaker's house,' I explained. 'The Education Board evidently didn't expect him to be home much.'

'Or to have anything major by way of a family or possessions.'

'At least it won't take long to pack up. I'm much more concerned about getting the last of the growing stock to the manor. As soon as the contractors bring the wrecking machine in next week, my poor bushes are going to be covered with brick and concrete dust.'

'Next *week*?'

I rubbed my nose. 'Yes, well, you don't have a monopoly on denial, you know. I kept expecting a last minute reprieve.'

He grinned at me. 'Tell me again why your family is so protective of you?'

I looked around for something to throw at him.

He caught my arm. 'No time. Let's get digging. Seriously though, about your family, you are one of the most competent people I know . . . '

'Apart from Coralie,' I said, leading the way outside and unlocking the toolshed.

'Apart from Coralie. Doesn't your family rate that?'

I ticked the reasons off on my fingers. 'I'm the youngest, most female, least academic and most prone to rushing into situations without considering the repercussions.'

'So, most caring, most practical, least self-aware aren't good qualities too?'

'Not in my mother's eyes. It's okay, Dad understands me. And Granny Annie. Theo, you don't have to help me. You have your own jobs to get on with.'

'The vegetables are done for the day,' he said. 'I want to get you moved in. No one should live somewhere this depressing, and apart from anything else, having Wild About Herbs visibly established at the manor will be another nail in Aunt Sue's coffin.'

The shifting of plants went vastly quicker with the two of us. I don't know whether it was the element of competition as to who could clear a patch first or just the fact that we were talking as we worked. Theo assessed my workshop while we were having a breather. 'We'll have a look when we get back to Wansdale and find a free room to set this lot up. You can choose somewhere permanent once Bruce moves out. I'm not sure myself how many odds and ends of rooms the manor has got.'

'Thanks. I keep forgetting you don't know your own gaff properly.'

He smiled. 'It's very weird exploring. I still haven't given up thoughts of finding the Wansdale Bounty. A treasure trove would take the edge off the urgency to make the manor pay for itself.'

'Strictly speaking,' I said, 'treasure trove is the property of the Crown. A hoard would suit you better. How do you know it hasn't already been found? The rhyme is centuries old.'

'There would be something about it in the family history. I've known the legend since I was a kid. My aunt is convinced of the treasure's existence. I'm sure that's why she wants to come over. She doesn't seem to have considered that with all the rewiring and plumbing the previous tenant did, anything stashed under the floorboards would be history by now. Aside from that possibility — which I admit is a big one — if the Bounty *had* been discovered, there'd be no need to keep passing the rhyme down through the generations, would there?'

'I suppose not. Unless one of your ancestors came across the hoard and lit out for pastures new without telling the rest of the family. Of course,' I added, 'the more we dig the old flower beds over, the more likely we are to come across buried treasure.'

'Even more reason to help you,' said Theo cheerfully.

* * *

It was a strange thing, but after spending all afternoon with Theo, I was oddly reluctant to call it a day. It's possible he was feeling the same.

'Don't you ever stop,' he said, looking

at me with a half-smile as I stood in the manor garden flexing my back and wondering which bed to tackle next. There weren't that many more plants to bring over now, but a couple of them were monsters.

'Not when things are going well,' I said.

'Hmm. Unlike you, my stomach is telling me my throat's been cut. I make a pretty mean stir fry if you fancy half of it?'

'Yes, but . . . ' I stopped, remembering I'd promised him a second massage.

'I've got plenty of veg, as you may have noticed.'

'Okay, then. Thank you.'

He wouldn't accept any help in the kitchen, so while he chopped and sizzled and splashed sesame oil around, I sat at his table with my laptop. I updated my website with my new address (which made the business sound about a hundred times more upmarket than previously) and added a photo of the herb dial as my new banner. I also created a rapid newsletter for my regulars giving the new address and warning that there might be a slight delay in processing orders. The postal list would have to wait until I could print the newsletter out, but the email customers could have theirs now.

'This is nice,' said Theo. 'I'd forgotten what it was like to have someone else in the house.'

I pressed the send icon and smiled at him over the top of my screen. 'Recluse syndrome strikes again. What will you do when your parents come home? Will you all shift across to the manor?'

'Don't know yet. They may want to stay on here. Seriously, Jen, I know your stock is important, but can we get you, yourself, moved in as soon as possible? The way the developers have left things, they might just as well have put a 'Welcome Vandals' mat down at the site entrance.'

That suited me fine. My plants were mostly in place and I wanted nothing more than to move to Wansdale. I wanted to walk out of my door every morning and see the garden falling in its lovely curves to the river. I wanted to cut down the willows and clear the brambles and make the shed properly mine. I'd wanted it from day one if I was honest.

'I'll ask Chris to hire a furniture-sized, self-drive van this weekend,' I said. 'It'll get him out of going home, which will please him. See, I'm emailing him now. That smells delicious, by the way.' And after the meal, I'd tell Theo to change into his shorts and I'd have a second go at his leg, whether he wanted me to or not.

I was ready for the twisty pain this time, felt it in my fingertips as soon as I touched the first of the comfrey cream to his scar. 'It feels cleaner,' I said. 'I can't believe you hung on to it for what five, six years?'

'Seven. Call me stubborn.'

Well, so was I, chasing down all the buried nerves and straightening them out. I heard my laptop chirrup the arrival of an email, but by then I was in a different world, so concentrated was I on navigating Theo's bungled injury. Which was . . . hard.

I frowned, analysing the problem. 'Theo, you need to let go of the wrongness. This is much harder work than last time.'

'I'm relaxed,' he protested, every sinew in his body giving me the lie.

'You so aren't. I'm pretty sure I only managed it before because I took your reflexes by surprise. They're ready for me today.'

'Balls. Sorry.'

'Tell me about your plans for the manor. What do you have to make out of it a year to cover the costs?'

'Assuming I don't have to pass over any of the takings to Aunt Sue?'

'If you had lived with my brother Anthony for as long as I have, you'd know that was a given. He's very good. Quite honestly, I'm amazed it's taken him this long to get back to you.'

As Theo talked, his body relaxed

enough to let me work. This was better. His enthusiasm for Wansdale and his love for its history filled him, allowing me to make long, probing sweeps all the way down the length of his scar.

His thigh, I thought, wouldn't need much more after this session. His calf, though, that had been horribly mangled in his fall. I closed my eyes, the better to sense the path of the injuries through bone and blood and muscle. My fingers worked his skin, pushing the healing oils through the epidermis, making deep passes down his leg. I wondered if there was another agent that would help to loosen the hard lump of scar. Honey, the lovely honey from his own beehives. Could I add honey to my salves? How would I stop it from . . .

'I said,' repeated Theo from a very long way away, 'that you should probably stop. You're practically asleep against the cushions.'

I pulled myself slowly out of his injury, aware of stiffness in my neck and a roughness against my temple and cheek, aware also that when I prised my eyes open the room swirled unsteadily around me. I closed them again, disorientated. I'd been sitting on the edge of the sofa to massage Theo's leg. I must have curled around and . . . 'Damn,' I said. 'I can't move.'

'I can't either. I'm not even going to ask what you were doing to my leg, but you've exhausted both of us fixing it. If I shuffle sideways, can you pull yourself along next to me so you can lie properly straight? You need to rest.'

Easier said than done. My body was as heavy as rolling water and twice as boneless. I slid down the sofa cushion, then hauled myself along the seat until my cheek rested against Theo's shoulder. His arm came around me and that was the last I remember until I woke again ninety minutes later feeling as if I'd just sat four finals back to back.

'Christ,' I said, not quite trusting myself to move any limbs. 'Next time, we might have to set a timer.'

Theo didn't open his eyes. 'No more

next times. My leg's on fire and you've burnt yourself out.'

'But does it feel better?'

'God knows. I'll tell you tomorrow.' He shifted his arm into a better position around me. 'Go back to sleep.'

I tried to formulate all the reasons why this was a lousy plan. I think I got as far as 'But . . . '

I was woken by a carillon of bells. A repeat carillon, getting louder each time. 'Oh God, my phone,' I groaned.

'Sorry,' said Theo, 'I can't reach it to turn it off.'

'It's okay.' I rolled across him and stumbled over to the table, picking up my phone and somehow managing to hit answer and loudspeaker together. 'Hi Chris,' I said, blinking at the display and wondering what time it was. I also wondered what day it was.

'Hi Jen. I've hired a van for Saturday, but we'll only have twenty-four hours because it's Granny Annie's seventy-fifth birthday on Sunday and we're due down there for lunch.'

I gave a faint whimper. 'It's her birthday this soon? I'd forgotten.'

'What I suggest is you pack as much as you can tonight and tomorrow, then we'll be ready to make the most of the day. Coralie says do you want to borrow her crates? She's got them piled up in one of the unused rooms at the manor.'

'Crates?'

'For packing. They're the ones she brought all the gear up in for the documentary. It's how normal people move house, Jen.'

'Oh. Yes, please.' I peered at Theo's clock. Ten o'clock and just light outside. Hopefully that meant ten o'clock tonight, not tomorrow morning. 'Is Coralie there, then?'

'Yes,' said my brother in the sort of voice that precludes any more questions.

'Okay, I'll, um, I'll see you Saturday morning. Thanks, Chris.' I put the phone down before I dropped it and realised my other hand was gripping the table to keep me upright.

'It seems I'll be moving in on Saturday,' I said. I looked at the clock again. 'Do you suppose this is still this evening?'

Theo shifted cautiously to the edge of the sofa and sat up. 'I think so. Bloody hell, Jen. Do you do that to all your patients?'

'Fall asleep on them, you mean? No, that's a first.'

He put his hand out and pulled me down to sit next to him. I was so weak it didn't take much of a tug. Resistance wasn't so much futile as impossible. 'No,' he said, 'do you always put so much into repair work. You're a danger to yourself.'

'Oh. No, that's a first too. I couldn't seem to stop.' The words set up an echo in my mind, but I was too knackered to trace it to its source. 'I should go home,' I said.

'Do you want to?'

I turned my head to meet his eyes. 'No, but I'm not sure I should stay here either.'

He was still holding my hand. He looked at our linked fingers. 'Do you want to?'

I moistened my lips. 'Stay here? Sort of.' There was a tiny silence. 'Theo, we haven't talked or . . . or anything. I should go.'

He swung his legs back on to the seat with a grunt. 'If you do, I'll be worrying about you all night and quite frankly, I could do with the sleep. You can crash on this sofa, or you can use one of the spare rooms. I'm damn sure you shouldn't be driving anywhere.'

It wasn't a very difficult decision to make. Right now I'd have trouble lifting the car keys to fumble them into the ignition. 'Okay,' I said meekly. 'Thank you. I don't suppose you have a bowl of soup about your person, do you?'

'There's some in the freezer.'

I considered the tasks involved in opening the freezer door, working out which tub the soup was in, putting it in the microwave and finally into a bowl. 'Bar of chocolate?' I asked.

'I'm not sure I could unwrap the silver foil.'

I nudged him sideways and wriggled down next to him. My bare leg rested against his scar. It felt clean and renewed and . . . and somehow joyful. 'The sofa is fine,' I said. And slept.

14

I woke to a pillow under my head, a light blanket covering me and a distinct lack of Theo. The time, I saw from my phone which had been thoughtfully placed on a small table by the sofa, was a quarter to five. There was also a note.

'*Good morning. I woke up feeling so much better that I thought it wisest to go to my own bed. Help yourself to tea. The crew usually arrive by seven.*'

Well, I thought, that neatly got around the difficulty of what to say to a person the morning after you'd slept with them but not *slept* with them. I ought to be equally tactful, even though part of me was quite keen to know what he'd have done if he *hadn't* chosen to be wise. As I'd realised the first time I'd treated his leg, you couldn't sink deep into a person's trauma and not be aware of their inner core. Theo's inner core was solid and warm, a far cry from the wary, detached man I'd met on my first day at Wansdale.

I folded the blanket, found my shoes and possessions, wrote *Thank you, see you later* on the note and let myself out. I needed a shower and a change of clothes before Coralie, and presumably by extension Chris, saw me next. Freedom of movement tended to only flow in one direction in our family.

It was while I was digging up the last of my big bushes that I heard the voices. Two men, sounding as if they were in my part of the school grounds. If they were customers, they were out of luck. I rounded the corner of my workshop to put them off, only to see one of them taking an axe to the door.

'Oi!' I yelled, adrenalin surging into me. 'What the hell do you think you're doing?'

They were both big men, in high-vis jackets. And there was an unmarked dirty red truck parked in my driveway facing the road. And I was small and female and rushing into unreconnoitred situations again. Without even thinking about it, my hand went to my pocket and swiped my phone. 'Call Theo,' I said. My earpiece crackled in reply. *Please, dear voice recognition, do not choose now to play up.*

'Contractors, love,' said the one with the axe. 'We're clearing the place before it gets knocked down.'

In my ear, I heard the immensely comforting sound of the ringing tone being replaced by Theo's voice. 'Hi Jen, where are you?'

'I'm afraid you've made a mistake,' I said crisply. 'This part of the site is still my property. Perhaps you should check with the office?'

'Yeah?' The bigger of the two moved towards me. I didn't like the way his gaze ranged casually over the buildings. 'That's not what I was told, love. All alone here, are you?'

'My partner is due back any minute,' I replied, stepping sideways so I could keep both of them in view. 'He's been out delivering. You'd better move your truck around to the main entrance or he'll block you in when he arrives.'

Both men's eyes flicked to the road.

'There's plenty of room in the car park,' I went on. 'Most of the businesses who were leasing space have vacated the premises. Only one or two left.'

There was a lot of swearing going on in my ear now, along with the sound of feet pounding on gravel. 'I'm there. For God's sake don't do anything stupid. Oh come on van, bloody start will you?'

The men exchanged a glance. The second one gave a shrug.

'Must be a cockup in the office,' said the first one. He lowered the axe and gave a look of cool professional dismissal at the damage he'd inflicted. 'Happens all the time. Useless gits. Sorry to have disturbed you, love.'

'I'll bet you are,' I muttered as I watched them swagger back to their truck. To my total lack of surprise, they drove past the old school entrance without pulling in. Five minutes after that, Theo's van hurtled into the spot they'd just vacated.

Several reactions hit me at once, including one I'd save to think about later.

'What happened? Are you all right?' Theo was out of the van in an instant, the door still swinging on its hinges as he burst over to me.

'Yes.' Shamefully, my knees buckled.

He caught me and held me close. 'Hey, I'm here. It's okay.'

For a moment, just for one moment, I allowed myself to feel weak and feeble and protected. 'You were right,' I said into his T-shirt. 'I need to move out as soon as I can. That was horrible. Two blokes. Looters, I think, dressed like workmen. They were going to break down the door. In broad daylight, Theo.'

Theo held me tighter, swearing comfortingly under his breath.

I swallowed. 'Do you . . . do you mind awfully giving me a hand again today? I'd quite like there to be somebody else about if they drive past again.'

'Try bloody stopping me.' He stiffened as he saw the gouges and splintered boards in the workshop door. 'I'm guessing you'd like to move your lab gear first? They meant business, didn't they?'

I nodded shakily. 'They had an axe.'

For a man who lived largely alone, Theo had an impressive range of curses in his vocabulary. 'You ring the police and your landlord,' he said when he'd run out of invective. 'I'll make tea, then one of us can go back to the manor for Coralie's crates to pack up your stuff.'

After I'd reported the attempted break-in and apologised for not getting a photo of the men or taking a note of the truck registration, I cradled my mug and met Theo's eyes. 'Thank you,' I said.

He slanted me an old-fashioned look. 'Oh come on, what was I supposed to do? Leave you to be raped and murdered while I finished hoeing the beans?'

'You could have finished dressing,' I said. 'Although I'm sure they'd have been terrified of you coming back from doing a delivery in your slippers.'

He looked down at his feet and chuckled. 'You can bring my boots when you collect the crates. I'll give you my key. One of us should definitely stay on the premises here. What did Chris mean, by the way?'

'When?'

'On the phone yesterday when he said crates were how normal people moved belongings?'

'I can't imagine. I mean, when I moved here I just bundled everything into my duvet cover and lobbed it in the van. It worked a treat.'

'You'd better not mention that to Coralie. She'll never recover. Workshop before house, then?'

I nodded. 'And there's the last half bed of herbs to finish. They're old and tatty but I don't want to leave anything here to be trashed.'

'Fair enough. You fetch the crates. I'll get digging.'

'In your slippers? Stop being so macho. You fetch the crates. I'll start dismantling the workshop. I'll bar the gate behind you.'

He looked at me carefully. 'Are you sure?'

'I'm sure.'

'Okay. Jen, about last night . . . '

'It's okay. We were both shattered.'

'Yes, but this morning I wasn't.'

I was unable to keep a sudden smile from my lips. 'Nor was I. I sort of wish you hadn't gone.'

He caught his breath. 'Really? You too?'

I nodded, feelings fluttering around in me like so many trapped moths. 'Um, later?' I managed.

'All right.' He gave me an awkward hug. 'I won't be long.'

We took it in turns for the rest of the day to move the last of my plants and my workshop crates. The heavy tools I propped up in my living room, the better for swiping at marauding intruders. Theo, it had to be said, was immensely better at packing up the equipment than I would have been. He'd found what I guessed had been a storage room next to the housekeeper's flat where we could set everything up again temporarily. For now, the crates went inside the door.

'You'll need to take all your light bulbs with you,' warned Theo. 'The tenants removed the existing ones when they went.'

'No. Really?'

'Petty, eh? I can understand them not wanting to leave the chandeliers up, but who the hell makes off with ordinary 60-watt bulbs when they are paying that much in rent?'

I briefly considered the likely number of rooms in the manor. 'Oh, I don't know. You don't get to be a millionaire by throwing away lights at two pounds fifty a pop.'

'Evidently.' He slid a look at me. 'Jen,

what time is Chris turning up with the van tomorrow?'

'Eight in the morning. I'm going to have to pack all night to be ready for him.'

'Would you like me to help? I'm really, really not keen on the thought of you being here on your own tonight, especially given your recent visitors.'

I stopped what I was doing, a great weight of relief rolling through me. 'I'd love you to,' I said.

'I'll pop over to the manor now and see to the chickens. Have you got any food here for tea?'

'Er, cheese?'

Theo opened the fridge door and looked inside. The silence was telling.

'Do you want to get fish and chips?' I looked around for my satchel. Where had I left it? It could be anywhere in this mess.

He kissed my forehead gently. 'I'll bring something back with me.'

Once I'd recovered from the shock of that kiss (which had set up a trail of fairly urgent reactions through my body), I stared at my living room in despair. Where to start?

One thing at a time, Jen, then move on to the next, it's not difficult.

I could almost hear Mum's impatient voice in my head. I gave up thinking and began to shift books out of bookcase number one into an empty crate. Chris would never let me hear the end of it if I was still packing when he arrived tomorrow morning.

*　*　*

'Don't look now, Jen, but I think we're done.'

'Can't be,' I said tiredly. 'There'll be another drawer, or a shelf, or a lurking cupboard that I filled up three years ago and haven't opened the door of since. How can a house this small have so much stuff?'

'I've checked. Just the sheets on your bed, the bathroom toiletries and the kitchen worktop.'

'Tell me we haven't packed the tea.'

'Don't be silly, I'm a gardener. I have to thank you, Jen. Without you working on my leg yesterday, I absolutely could not have done that.'

I blinked at him in astonishment. 'You're thanking me? Theo, without you I'd still be on the first bookcase. I'm so grateful I can't find the words.'

He came over and linked his arms around me. 'I'm not sure I want gratitude.'

I looked at him, the excitement I'd been keeping at bay all day building in me. His touch, even this casually, was doing all sorts of things to my body. More importantly, what I *wasn't* getting was a bombardment of emotion. Maybe it was dependent on what I felt for the boy, rather than what he felt for me.

I just had to make sure of one thing. 'This isn't payment for the healing, is it?

'No, it bloody isn't!'

'Good,' I said, and kissed him. And lo, it was stupendous.

It was a very, very good thing that we were both accustomed to dawn starts. As it was, we were chastely loading the open-this-first kitchen box into my van when Chris arrived ten minutes early. Considering what we'd been up to already this morning, this was quite some feat. Mind you, Coralie matched us for insouciance as she hopped down from the cab with a preliminary loading plan on the screen of her tablet.

'Not working this weekend?' I asked her.

She did turn a little pink at that. 'Bruce is going to Mrs M's medieval banquet, so I told him I was in danger of burning out unless I also had some me time. As soon as the actors arrive on Monday we'll be working a full-on seven day week.'

'Then a weekend off sounds very wise,' I replied with a straight face. 'Thank you, Coralie.'

She grinned at me. 'He was so

shocked. It was wonderful.'

I grinned back. Love (or at least sex) seemed to have adjusted her inferiority complex nicely. I have to admit, as a director of operations, she was marvellous. I was installed in the housekeeper's flat, books unpacked, my clothes hung up and the furniture disposed about the rooms in the optimal feng shui arrangement long before nightfall and quicker by two or three weeks than if I'd been left to myself. She even got us all showered and changed and around a table in the local Indian restaurant before they took the final orders of the evening.

'To Coralie,' I said, raising my beer. 'If I ever move again, I want you right there with your tablet.'

She blushed as we all chinked glasses. 'Thank you,' she said. 'What time are we setting off tomorrow?'

Say what?

'I've asked Coralie to come with us to Granny Annie's birthday lunch,' said Chris, meeting my eyes. His fingers did the tiniest drum roll on the table.

This was evidently the price of his help today. Ah well, I was happy to take the heat off them by offering myself up as a sacrificial lamb. 'Fantastic,' I said. 'Not that you'll be able to get a word in edgeways with me telling Mum all about Wansdale and my new gaff.'

Chris smiled a thank you and his hand drifted sideways to clasp Coralie's.

'What are your sisters-in-law like?' she whispered to me.

'Ewan's Clare is adorable,' I murmured. 'Anthony's Gina is . . . is the sort of person who uses ready-made Perrier ice cubes.'

Coralie's face cleared. 'Oh, like Rosamund. I can deal with that.'

Theo cleared his throat. 'I suppose there isn't room for another one in your car, mate?' he asked. 'I'm getting the hang of this anti-recluse idea now.'

Bless him, Chris's eyes nearly fell out of his head. 'Yes, absolutely,' he said, looking from me to Theo in wild surmise. Beside him, Coralie's face was a triumph in not looking smug.

'Are you sure?' I said to Theo. 'There are likely to be an awful lot of us. It's Granny's seventy-fifth, so I should think Uncle Bill and my cousins and their partners will all be there to help her celebrate too.'

He smiled at me. 'I'll have to meet them sometime, won't I?'

My head whirled, trying to contain the excited little bunny-hops my chest was doing. 'I guess,' I said, and couldn't think of anything else to say at all. Oh, wait, yes I could. 'I haven't got Granny a card yet, Chris,' I said. 'Can we stop at a service station on the way?'

15

Chris and I couldn't have organised it better if we'd planned it for months. Mum was simultaneously delighted and furious with us. Delighted because all of her children briefly had wonderfully boastable-about partners. Furious because this was Granny Annie's day and she couldn't in all conscience spare the time to find out every single possible detail about Coralie and Theo. Also frustrated because she was having to pretend to Uncle Bill and the cousins that this hadn't come completely out of the blue and she'd known all along.

Eventually she cornered Chris and Coralie under the pretext of writing something nice in the family photo album she'd put together for Granny. I extracted Theo from where he and Anthony were having a lovely talk about family trust documents and we went over to sit with Granny herself.

'I hope you don't want intelligent con-versation,' I said to her. 'I've been moving for the last three days and I'm knack-ered.' I frowned as I kissed her cheek. 'But not too knackered to give your shoulder a rub.' I moved behind her chair and began a very delicate massage of the big muscle across her shoulder. It was a problem she'd had for years. Every now and again she managed to twist awkwardly and it flared up again.

'No stamina, you kids today,' teased Granny. 'If you'd grown up in a log cabin in the middle of the prairies like I did, you'd laugh at a handful of mere twelve hour days.'

'You must be where Jen gets it from,' said Theo with a smile. 'I've yet to see her do as little as twelve hours in a day.'

'And you're any better?' I asked him with eyebrows raised.

He grinned. 'Whereabouts did you grow up, then?' he asked Granny.

'Manitoba. We're all tough stock. My grandparents had the only homestead for miles that prospered during the Depression instead of going under.'

'That sounds intriguing,' said Theo. 'How did they manage it?'

I smiled as I very slightly increased the pressure in my fingers. Maybe you could tell a man by his manners. Theo's were beautiful.

'Ah, well, the price of wheat went down and down after the stock market crash, so there were no wages for the men for most of the thirties and of course no medical care without paying for it. But my grandma used to be a nurse, so she kept everyone healthy and knew what vitamins and so on needed adding to the food. Folk who'd been laid off at other farms all showed up and the way my grandpa told it, he never turned anyone away. He was a very clever man. He organised the families into building their own shacks and cooking communally. He stored the grain against the future. He kept the books straight and encouraged everyone to think like a community and pull together. He'd already been running a small school for the children about the place, and now he taught the parents to read and write too, which stood them in good stead when the Second World War came and the economy picked up. By the time I was toddling around the settlement and taking notice after the war, not one of us kids were hungry or ignorant or didn't have a new set of clothes twice a year.' She paused. 'It was still bloody cold though. Even Grandma and Grandpa couldn't fix that.'

'So you got married to an Englishman the first moment you could and moved with him to the UK,' I said with a laugh.

She chuckled. 'I did. Never regretted it. Whenever I wrote home, I used to tell the family how wonderful it was here. Mum used to get dreadfully travel sick, so I knew she'd never shift. Once was enough for her. Laurel didn't believe me enough to visit. Thought I was making it up at first. Youngest one, you see. Never could do anything right.

Thank you, darling, that's feeling easier already.'

'You should have said your shoulder was hurting as soon as I got here. Have you asked Dad about it?'

'He told me to ask you for a rub, dear.'

Theo chuckled. 'Keeping it in the family.'

'We always do,' said Granny. 'Jen gets it from my grandma. Every time any of us hurt ourselves as children, we'd go to her and she'd have us better in an instant.'

I kissed her. 'Comfort is what grannies are for. I'd love to chat more, but I promised Chris I'd run interference for him and here I am nattering to you instead. Do you fancy looking at some old family photos, Theo?'

'Bet you anything you like they are just like mine.'

'Probably. Speak to you later, Granny. I'll tell Chris you are dying to meet his young lady. Actually, she's a friend of mine and very nice.'

I was prepared to put up with Mum's questions, really I was, but just as we circulated ourselves over there, Dad mentioned something smelling as if it was burning in the kitchen and took her place at the photo album.

I smiled at him. 'Thanks.'

'Thanks, nothing. What's your diagnosis of Granny's shoulder?'

I wrinkled my nose. 'It feels as though there may be a spur on the bone. I've suggested to it that it stops growing, and I've reduced the inflammation. I'll come over again in a couple of weeks if you like? Or you could drive her up to Wansdale. I'd love to show you the garden.'

'Now that's a good plan,' said Dad, pleased, 'and it won't look as if we're fussing. I really don't want an operation for her.'

Theo had tactfully opened the album so he couldn't hear an experienced family GP asking his daughter to practise witchcraft on his mother. 'Ah yes,' he said. 'As I thought. Just like my family's old photos, except the background is different. I wouldn't exactly describe your granny's house as a log cabin though.'

I looked and smiled. I'd seen the photo before, but I'd forgotten it. On the verandah of a sprawling farmhouse were ranged Granny and her older sister as remarkably cute little moppets, her mother and father smiling behind them, and standing laughing on either side, her grandma & grandpa. Her grandma had slacks on and a garden fork in her hand as if she'd been digging. Her grandpa was leaning on his stick.

'I can see where you get your hair from,' Theo said with a grin.

It was true. Granny's mum had a bandeau around a shock of hair just like mine. I wondered if it was the same colour. It was difficult to tell in black and white.

'The other difference,' said Theo,

tapping the photo, 'is that my family would be posed stiffly against the manor, all dressed in their very best, even during the war. Not a smile amongst them. Your lot look much friendlier.'

Granny had been listening. 'Laughed the whole time,' she confirmed. 'Let me see it, Jen.'

I got out my phone to take a photo of the cheerful group, then carried the book over. 'Who are the people in this other photo, Granny?' I asked. 'Don't you all look smart. Was it a special occasion?'

It had evidently been taken ten years or so after the first one as Granny and her sister were now young teenagers.

'Oh yes,' she said. 'That was Grandma and Grandpa's fortieth wedding anniversary. They didn't usually make a fuss about celebrations, but one of my uncles had won a competition in the paper and the prize was a family party in a hotel in Winnipeg, all expenses paid. That's me and Laurel in our new dresses. My mother had a new frock too. Then those are my uncles looking very debonair and their wives, and all my cousins. My word, how I adored that hotel. That was the evening I realised there was more to life than a farm in the middle of nowhere. It did my schoolwork no end of good. I decided I was going to be a city secretary if it killed me.' She nodded at the photo. 'Laurel gave me the photo when I married and moved to London. She said I'd need something to remember the family by.'

'Laurel's your sister?' asked Theo. 'Have you seen her at all since you left?'

'We Skype most weeks,' said Granny matter-of-factly. 'Life's much easier with email. It used to take forever exchanging news by letter. The Manitoba mail service leaves a lot to be desired.'

Theo grinned. 'But you've not been back?'

'Why would I need to? Some of my cousins have been over at various times, and Ewan stayed with one of the younger set at the university when he went out there a while back for work.

Cousin John's boy, Max, I think it was. I forget all their names.'

I took a photo of this picture too. It was in colour, showing that Granny's mum's hair had indeed been the same sandy shade as mine.

'Throwbacks, the pair of us,' said Dad, seeing where I was looking. He touched his own thinning crop ruefully.

'Lunch is ready,' called Mum. 'Come and help me carry it through.'

As we all made an exodus to the dining room, I reflected that Granny had created a clan of her own every bit as large and happy as the one she'd left behind in Canada. But now she was the oldest rather than the youngest.

'What are you thinking about?' said Theo.

'Families. Cycle of life. One day not being the youngest.'

Theo gave a lopsided grin. 'I'm coming around to the idea myself.'

★ ★ ★

Monday. I woke up in my new bedroom for the first time. I also woke up next to Theo.

'Mmm,' he said, running his hand over me. 'This is nice.'

'It is,' I agreed. 'What time did Coralie say the film crew were arriving? Should I move my van around to your side to be out of the way?'

He opened his eyes reproachfully. 'You had to spoil it. Good idea about the van. Park it next to mine.' He stretched. 'Something seems to have given me an appetite. Do you want to come over to my place for breakfast?'

I kissed him. It still felt very new, very special. 'Give me half an hour to shower and dress.'

In fact, I only needed ten minutes. The rest of the time was spent hunting for the writing slope. This was the trouble with letting other people unpack for you. I'd been going to present it to Theo as a family heirloom in return for the bacon and eggs. Now I had to resign myself to either not finding it for another three months or swallowing my pride and ask Coralie where in her opinion a writing desk ought to live. I did like her, honestly, but I had the lowering feeling that if she and Chris stayed together it was going to be just like having a slightly bossy sister.

Association of ideas is a weird thing. As I drove the van around to the dower house, I realised what had been niggling at me since yesterday. Granny saying her grandpa had started a school on their land. But I distinctly remembered her telling me a different story when I was younger. It hadn't struck me at the time, because to me at that age, Granny's stories were tales of a different world, all of them equally alien to a young millennial growing up in suburban London. It puzzled me now though. I'd been spending the day with Granny because it was the holidays and Dad was working and Mum was on a course, or teaching a course, or something. And the boys were at some sort of sporty holiday thing and I wasn't and it wasn't fair.

'It's the lot of the youngest to be left behind,' Granny had said. 'It was the same when I had to walk anywhere with Laurel. She was taller than me and used to walk twice as fast. I swear my left arm is longer than my right to this day because of being towed behind her so often when I was small.'

I'd laughed, imagining a cartoon Granny with different length arms.

She'd looked at me approvingly. 'That's better. And my mother told me that when she first started at the village school, her older boy cousins who were supposed to take her would let go of her hand as soon as they were out of sight of the house and run off down the road, leaving her to plod after them by herself. Boys are frequently mean. Shall we make a cake?'

And we had made the cake, and I'd conscientiously saved slices for Ewan and Anthony and Chris, and I'd thought no more about the story. But now . . .

'The thing is,' I said to Theo over a thoroughly glorious breakfast, 'Granny has never, ever mentioned any other branches of the family. Just her grandma and grandpa on their homestead, and her mother and two uncles, then her and Laurel and all their cousins. So where did these *older* cousins of her mum come from? And why would her grandpa have needed to start a school of their own if there was a village school already there?'

'For that matter,' said Theo, his eyes thoughtful, 'a village itself doesn't sound right, does it? Didn't she call it a settlement yesterday? I thought the prairies consisted of huge farms with acres of fields, and small townships dotted about for trade.'

'I don't know. I hadn't thought of that. I'll ask her next time I talk to her.' I smiled at him, overcome with a flood of pleasure that here was a man who was clever, but not pushy over breakfast. A man who'd put up with my family yesterday without complaint. A man who . . .

'What are you thinking?' he asked.

I hastily modified my expression. 'Nothing. I'm just wondering if you are a wash-up-as-you-go person or a leave-it-until-the-end-of-the-day merchant.'

He looked at me straight faced. 'I generally put everything in the dish-washer until it's full, then get out the instruction booklet. Do you want help setting up your stills and presses and things?'

'No, I'm okay.' I stretched up and kissed him. 'This is nice.'

'It is. See you later.'

16

The manor was a changed environment now the actors and all the associated crew were here. Busier, noisier, taking on a different character as people jockeyed subtly for their own few square feet of home space. I could see why Bruce had wanted to film the cutaway scenes in advance. I retreated to my workroom, fixed my *Wild About Herbs: Private* sign from the school site to the door and kept well out of the way. I had just about set everything up when I got a call from Theo.

'I'm starving. Do you want to try the catering truck?'

'Love to. Where is it?'

'Out at the front. You can't miss it. There's a queue all the way to the stable block. I'm saving you a place.'

I walked around the side of the house and stopped in shock. Since this morning, the front lawns had sprouted picnic benches and tables. The drive was now solid with vehicles. 'Crikey,' I said inadequately to Theo. 'This is even more people than I'm used to.'

'Tell me about it. What do you say to taking our plates of lasagne down to the chickens? I can let the bees know what's going on.'

'Good idea. And on the way we can talk about pollarding your willows for our mutual benefit.'

His mouth, which had been looking a bit set, quirked into a grin. 'Mutual?'

'I get light in the shed and bark for willow bark tea, you get twigs and withies and logs.'

'Seems reasonable. Is it something Bruce might want to film?'

I felt a guilty jolt. 'Oh, drat. Yes, probably. I was just thinking about my own business. Are we going to have to wait until Coralie can find us a moment with Fran? That could take a while.'

'He'd appreciate it though, don't you think? And this helpful cooperation of ours works two ways. We could ask him for say a sixty second video each of the work we do. He's got plenty of footage of us by now, they must be able to edit something together that we can use as adverts.'

We'd reached the beehives. I sat on the bench next to him almost struck dumb with amazement. 'Theo, that's a brilliant idea.'

'It is, isn't it? Time was I'd have thought of it the second day he was here. What the hell have I been doing with my brain for the past few years?'

'Letting it heal?'

'Nice try. I'd shut it down, Jen.'

'You can't hurry trauma-recovery. It was healing. Eat your nice lasagne.'

Some of the hens came fussing over, one or two hopping up to the bench in a great flutter of feathers so they could peck inquisitively at our plates.

Theo fended them off. 'You've given me back my life,' he said flatly.

'Well, it did seem an awful waste having it lying around, not being used,'

I replied. 'Stop this, Theo. I can't help mending people when I feel something wrong, you can't help being clever, even when you're hiding from the world. You'd have got there by yourself eventually. I just pressed the accelerator pedal.'

'That's another thing. It should have been a dead man's handle. Nature forgot to fit you with an off switch.'

'Are you complaining?'

'I don't know. I don't know what I am. I'm grateful and appalled in equal measure. And I'm being bad-tempered and I don't mean to be.'

'You don't like being beholden. Sorry. You kind of get used to things being done for you, whether you want it or not, in my family.'

'I can't resent you fixing me, Jen. But it scares me how much you put into it.'

And that, I realised in a lightning rush, was what made him different.

'Yes, well, that's why I don't work in hospitals,' I said. 'I do feel guilty, but Dad says it's about picking your battles and applying talent where it can do the most good. I don't know if I could save a life, I've never been in that position. I'm pretty sure I'd wind up unconscious if I had to try. What I mostly do is help people carry on as normal. It doesn't bother me if they don't realise I'm doing it. Why are you not telling the bees about the filming?'

He grinned at me in a shamefaced way that stirred my blood nicely. 'I told them first thing this morning. I just wanted to be alone somewhere with you while we ate.'

I leant against his shoulder, completely melted inside. 'Now look what you've done. I've gone all tingly. I ought to get on. I've got so much work piling up it's not true. I've just thought, if Fran can edit me a tiny film, I can put it on my website to prove all my stuff is artisan-made by me, not a factory. My customers will love it. I've had emails already wishing me luck with the move.'

'Sweet of them. Have you got a large customer base?'

'Enough so it's a bit of a hop when

they all order at once. My dear brothers have business cards that they scatter around the country for me. Not that I ever asked them to. They just do it. Damn, I've just realised I'm going to have to order new cards with this address and I no longer have a printing firm next door. And I need to print out newsletters for the snail mail people. I'll do that as soon as I get back to the house. Tell you what, once you get your manor-for-hire business up and running, I'll include a disguised advert for it in my mailing. Shall I plug your veg boxes too? Do you ever ship them?'

'The postage would be more than the contents are worth.'

'Forget that for an idea then. Where's the nearest post office? In the village? Are the people nice? I'll be putting a fair amount of traffic their way.'

'Yes, they're nice. It's incorporated into the shop-and-dry-cleaner. Go into the village, then first left past the re-purposed school, can't miss it.'

'Thanks. I'll introduce myself and get

the newsletters posted, then devote the rest of the afternoon to gardening.'

'You really don't ever stop, do you? Do you want me to pull the hose over?'

I smiled at him. 'Don't you need it yourself? You are a treasure.'

He kissed my nose. 'I'm honestly not. See you later.'

I smiled to myself as I hurried back to my flat and hunted for wherever Coralie thought envelopes ought to be stored. I wasn't sure what Theo and I had, and I really hoped it wasn't just gratitude on his part, but it was rather lovely to be going on with.

★   ★   ★

I had printed, enveloped and posted the newsletters. I had checked on my plants and firmed in the ones I'd been a bit hasty with on Saturday. I'd ventured up to the catering truck for a carton of tea and now I was sitting on the step of the shed sipping it while I grew accustomed to the sight of people in WW1 clothes drifting around on the terrace. Occasionally Coralie scooted across, gathering them up and emptying the scene for a while.

I leaned against the door frame and realised with a rush of pleasure that I'd found the writing slope. I must have tucked in back into its space days ago and forgotten I'd done it. I looked up at the rafters. Yes, the key was pressed into the knothole.

I fetched the desk out, unlocked it, lifted the diary carefully and started reading from where I'd left off. The next entry was very short and much blotched, as if Louise had wept over the page. As my eye accustomed itself to her writing, I realised that was exactly what she'd done.

Dreadful day. Dreadful, dreadful day. Freddy has been killed. It happened in Flanders, which I have always thought of as such a peaceful place. Mother and Father are beside themselves with grief. I am scarcely less so. At least Edmund still lives. We hope.

Oh no. I felt my own heart catch at Louise's pain. The tea grew cold as I read on. There was nothing for a couple of days, then,

I cannot bear Geraldine this week. She has always considered herself superior, but now she glides about the house with a new light in her eye. 'This will be mine,' I can see her thinking as she rests her hand on the sideboard holding the best dinner service. 'And this. And this,' as she straightens the linen and rotates a wineglass in her hand. Oh, how I wish Freddy had not been a gentleman and had married Lucy Carlisle before he left. At least then there might be a small Freddy to take the shine out of Geraldine's bearing. As it is, Wansdale will go to Edmund when Father dies, and to Richard after that. Already, Mother and Geraldine are treating Richard differently from his brother, for William will now only come into whatever of

Geraldine's settlements are left after her making such a show of mourning. She and Mother have entered into what Archie Wright calls armed neutrality. One has the power, the other the power-in-waiting. I escape to the ward or the stillroom or the garden as much as possible. As soon as the war is over, I will go to London or Manchester and find a job. I won't be able to bear it here.

Poor, poor Louise. How awful for a sensitive girl to be caught between such inflexible personalities. I turned the page.

I did my nursing shift today, for it is wrong to shirk responsibility and indulge my misery when these brave men have risked all for us, whatever Geraldine says. It left me so tired that it must have been visible, for Robbie Gibbs again came after me to offer his help in the garden. He is nearly recovered, but whilst Archie is still unwell and immobile, he is allowed to stay here and is a great help on the ward. So many of the men need restraining in the night, or supporting during the day. Today he helped me harvest wintergreen leaves from under the willow. I must remember to gather the seed this year and sow some more further up the bank, for it is proving most useful. I told him how the plant decides for itself where it will grow and where it will not and he laughed and said he had known some people like that. After we had done that, he dug over almost half a bed before he returned to the house. Mother's vases this year will not be as abundant as usual but I need the ground for feverfew and valerian. The valerian in particular is proving to be a blessing in calming some of the men. Never would I have believed the disturbances to the brain this war has caused had I not seen it for myself. Robbie is the most restful person to work with. I found myself telling him about Freddy, and feeling better by remembering all the good, kind things he ever did. When I said I wished he had married Lucy as they had planned, Robbie looked troubled. 'It is a difficult choice, following your heart or behaving with honour. Your brother will have been comforted, knowing that he was doing the right thing, as he saw it, by leaving her free.'

I argued that surely it was different in times of war when one might be killed — not that any of them thought they would when they marched off — and asked if he had a wife or sweetheart at home, and if he had had to make a choice. I was sorry I'd been so sharp when he blushed to his hairline, saying that he had not yet met a young lady he felt he could share his life with, for as long as that life might be. I thought, as I have done before, that Archie is very lucky to count Robbie as a friend.

So this was Robbie. I could see why he appealed to Louise. I shifted to the facing page and gave a tiny gasp as I read the next words.

Robbie has made me a writing desk to fit snugly under the bench of the shed. He is a carpenter at home, and finds it impossible to be idle. He has been mending chairs and replacing all my tool handles, and saved these scraps of wood so that I would have somewhere to store my secrets away from Mother's busy eyes. I will miss him when he is sent back.

Louise was falling in love. I recognised the signs. Unfortunately, a gentleman's daughter and an estate carpenter was an impossible match in 1915. I leafed forward.

Today has had a silver lining after all. Robbie had received orders to return, but this morning he came to me in great distress with raised weals and blisters all over his arms and chest, for all the world as if he had been badly burned. We were at a loss to account for them, until I remembered he helped with harvesting the rue yesterday and I recalled we once had a housemaid who had the same reaction when she handled rue plants.

Ouch. I shuddered in sympathy for poor Robbie. He must have been the one Louise had made the chamomile lotion for in the script. I looked up, my eyes going across the herb dial to my own stand of rue plants. Rue was good for headache relief and sweating out a fever, but it was a nightmare if you were allergic to it. I couldn't go anywhere near it without gloves up to my armpits and it was even worse in the sunshine, for some reason. That was why I'd sited these plants at the back with a warning label. I returned to the diary. Presumably Robbie had recovered?

Blessings really do come in disguise. The doctor pronounced Robbie unable to travel for a week. I soothed his blistered skin with chamomile, self-ishly glad that he would be here a little longer, and as I did so, I could feel his heart and I understood without words what it was he felt for me yet didn't dare say. Such quiet, intense joy as my eyes met his I have never known before. It is too commonly said, but our hearts did for a few moments beat as one. We are to meet this evening down by the herb dial, alone.

Which they had. With results never even hinted at in the documentary. The war, apparently, had made their choice for them.

Whoa. I leaned back against the door frame of the shed, full of a rush of emotion that I didn't understand. I knew — of course I knew — that people had been having sex before marriage for centuries. I also knew Louise was a modern woman for 1915 and was constantly rebelling against her constraints. So when love came, whoosh, it swept her away. But . . . but she'd married Archie. I turned back to her diary with trepidation.

Robbie has asked me to marry him. Of course I will. I would marry him today, but he must return to Flanders and does not want my life here to be even more intolerable than it is already. Reluctantly, I have promised that I will not tell anyone about us. He brought me letters of such love before he left. I have hidden them in his desk and given him a pot of Wansdale honey to remind him of me. I pray he will use it on his own wounds if he is hurt again, but I know him too well not to expect him to also smear it on comrades when necessary. He is the very best of men. I never thought to know such happiness as this. I am so very lucky.

Robbie, however, had not been lucky. He had been caught in enemy gunfire within the week whilst rescuing a colleague. Louise's grief had spilled over two full pages of the diary. And then she had realised she was pregnant. I had tears running down my own cheeks as I read on.

I am happy — how could I not be — that I will after all have something of Robbie, but my heart is heavy at what I must do. Yesterday, Archie proposed to me. A week ago I would have declined gently and told him about Robbie. They were friends and grew up together, for all they were different classes. Things are now different. I have more than just myself to think of. I like Archie very much. Had I never known Robbie, I would have accepted him without thinking twice. I do believe I can come to love him properly once my grief subsides. At any rate, I will make him the best wife any man could ask for and he will never, ever know he was not my first love. But it must be soon. Once again, the war will be my excuse — and my salvation.

The final diary entry had been written on her wedding eve.

I find I cannot use this box any longer. It divides my heart too much. I'll leave it in the place he made for it. No one comes in here now except me, so it will be safe enough.

Tomorrow I restart life as Mrs Archie Wright. We are to remain at Wansdale, until at least the end of the war. There is no place for him on his brother's small estate, but here there is work to spare for both of us. After that, who can tell what shape the world will be? My dreams are now in Archie's hands, under Archie's stars. I must and will be loyal to him. He has grand visions and the intelligence and drive to make them a reality. I pray I will prove worthy.

I closed the diary and locked it back into the little desk. There were letters underneath it, and sprigs of rosemary. I didn't touch them. I ought to give the desk to Theo, but Louise was in my soul now. I knew she and Archie had emigrated, but until I knew what had become of Robbie's child, I couldn't betray her great secret. How to find out, though? Unless there was another diary somewhere deeper in the shed?

★　★　★

Reading Louise's journal had left me horribly unsettled. The manor felt far too full of people and every time one of the actors crossed my field of vision in a WW1 uniform I jumped, thinking I was seeing Robbie's or Archie's ghost. When Theo texted me to ask if I wanted to eat at his house this evening rather than my flat, I very nearly broke the land-speed record locking up and dashing next door.

We didn't talk at all about injuries or talents or what either of us had or hadn't done with our lives. Theo found a bottle of wine and we made grand, ridiculous plans for the manor and went to bed early in total harmony.

I fitted my leg naturally to his scar before we slept, and I dreamt I was Louise covering Archie's damaged body with her own, mending him night after night with the love in her growing belly, binding the three of them together to make a strong future.

17

'Do you suppose it would be cheeky,' said Theo as we gazed out of his bedroom window to where the catering truck was already dispensing bacon rolls, 'if we got breakfast from the truck and brought it back here to eat?'

'It sounds an excellent idea to me. Are you doing anything special today?'

'Restaurant order to crate up, followed by a little light weeding. Why?'

'Come and find me in the garden later. I've got something to show you.'

He pretended to look shocked. 'In broad daylight? With the cast looking on?'

'This is something else,' I said, swatting him gently. 'Something different. But I need to show it to you down by the shed.' Whether it was the dream or just the knowledge that Theo and I were growing closer I didn't know, but

I'd woken in his arms with the absolute certainty that he too needed to read Louise's diary. She was his several times great aunt. The box was his property. And I didn't want to have any secrets from him.

Later, when I looked up from tidying the lavender and saw him walking across from his barn, my heart gave an unexpected flip. I still didn't know quite how he felt about me, but I was beginning to know exactly what it was I felt for him.

'Go on then,' he said. 'If it's the Wansdale Bounty, I forgive you the secrecy.'

'It's not. Sorry. It's the writing slope I've been using. It came from the shed.'

'Jen, I'm not going to begrudge you a wedge of wood.'

I drew him over to the open door and pointed. 'It was made for Louise. Look there — the hiding place for it was crafted specially. Her journal was it.'

'And?' His eyes were intelligent, but puzzled.

'Louise's story isn't how Bruce has written it,' I said, sliding the writing desk out. I reached up to the fake knot hole for the key. 'I found the desk first and the key later. Read it. Read it here where she wrote it. It's yours. I should have told you before.'

I finished stringing up bunches of lavender for drying. Bruce wanted more for the stillroom set, and I needed some for myself anyway. Bees moved purposefully overhead. I heard the tiny rustle of paper as Theo turned a page.

'Wintergreen!' I said aloud. 'I never did look. Louise said it grew under the willow in her day.'

'Pardon?' said Theo, not really hearing me.

'English wintergreen. Louise gathered it in the diary, so the ground evidently used to suit it down near the water. Even if there's none there now, I should be able to clear a bit of space to plant my own. I'm going to have a hunt around. Carry on reading. If you hear a splash it'll only be me falling in the river.'

'Okay, love. Be careful of that broken jetty.'

Love? My head snapped around to him, but he was a hundred years back in the past and clearly had no idea what he was saying. Calm down, Jen. I rounded the shed and ducked under the willows to pick my way through the nettles. It was going to be a positive pleasure to harvest these in the fullness of time.

I'd only gone a few yards before I saw, within a dense tangle of brambles, a delicate white spike of bells, maybe a foot high, rising from a circle of long-stemmed, round green leaves.

'Wintergreen,' I breathed, my eyes probing the thicket and making out further nodding white stems leading sporadically to the river. I stayed there, not moving, just drinking in the will-o'-the-wisp ghost flowers with my eyes.

Behind me I heard Theo's footsteps coming through the undergrowth. 'It's Louise's wintergreen,' I whispered. 'Look at it all. Do you know how scarce this is in the wild? Sorry, Theo, you're never going to get rid of me now. It's the perfect habitat, right on my doorstep.'

Gathering it would be a challenge, mind, but I'd worry about that later.

'Really? That's brilliant. I'd like to say it was Louise, leaving it for you, but I'm afraid it was sheer neglect in the first instance, then the tenants wanting privacy at the expense of tidiness in the second. Is that the wound-herb you used on me?'

'Yes, it's probably just as well the plants are there since I'm going to get hacked to pieces clearing the brambles away so I can reach them.'

'Ironically self-defeating, using up a rare plant on yourself just so you can get to the rare plant. Louise would never approve.'

'You finished the diary, then?'

'I did.' He wrapped his arms around me and held me close. For a moment we stood there, at one with the garden. I didn't need to ask if we should tell Bruce, with his passion for accuracy, that his script was wrong. The answer would be a no.

'I want to know more,' I confessed as

we emerged from the shade of the willows. 'I want to know if she had the baby. I want to know if she was happy.'

'We could ask Barbara again. Louise used to write to Lady Mary.'

'Barbara would have said if the letters had been saved. I did wonder if Louise kept a journal after she got married. Maybe I could google her? All sorts of things get put on the internet.' I got out my phone and keyed in 'Louise Wright diary journal'.

LOW BATTERY, it flashed back at me.

'Ooops,' I said. 'I forgot to charge it last night. I wonder why?'

'Can't imagine,' said Theo with a straight face. 'Try googling from the research room. After reading the diary, I've got this nagging memory about a photo in Coralie's collection.'

'What sort of photo?'

'I'll tell you when I've found it. You're not the only one who can do mysterious.'

While Theo rummaged through the

trays of ephemera, I dumped my lavender on a table, took the strung bunches to the stillroom, then came back and typed in my query again. There were masses of Louise Wrights. I added 'emigration' to the search bar, thinning down the results dramatically. Nothing on the first page, so I clicked on the next and, 'Theo,' I gasped. 'I think I've found her.' I didn't even look at the citation or which web page it was from, just read the entry.

The text said, *Louise Wright was a prolific journal keeper, starting from the early days of her emigration from England in 1923.* The photo next to it showed a facsimile page from a journal, written in a neat hand I knew very well indeed. I zoomed in on the image, straining to make out the words.

March 1923: I write this on deck. Ian is on my lap, solemn and alert at the bustle of the ship, but Archie, Dorothy and Jack are below and unwell. Dorothy is suffering the worst. Her seasickness is acute. I have persuaded her to swallow a little ginger and honey linctus and hope she will soon be her sunny self again. Time is extraordinary. I can't believe it was only a week ago that we corded the final trunk and closed the dower house door for the last time. It seems longer, as if in our hearts we left a long time ago. This is the last time I will ever look back. Today is the beginning of a new life. Already, despite the close confines of this ship and the sickness, I feel truly free.

'It is her,' I said. 'Theo, it is! She and Archie lived in your house when they were first married.' I stabbed the link with an impatient click.

The hourglass rotated leisurely. Theo's phone suddenly bellowed from his pocket.

'Hi, Coralie,' he said, thumbing the loudspeaker icon. 'What's up?'

Coralie's voice was crisp and unarguable with. 'There is a loud, aggressive woman in the Great Hall demanding to see you. She needs to be out of here *now*, Theo. Ten minutes ago would be good.'

His face clouded. 'Bloody hell. Okay, I'm there.' He put the phone and the photo he'd been holding into his pocket and reached out his hand for me. 'It's Aunt Sue. Has to be. Come on. I need back up.'

I rapidly emailed the Louise diary link to myself, scooped up my sheaf of lavender and ran after him.

'The manor is let, Aunt Sue,' he was saying forcefully to a middle-aged, rigidly tailored woman, when I caught up. 'We have to get out of the way. Come next door and let's talk this over civilly, please.'

'This is my family home,' the woman was saying stubbornly. 'I've got the right to be here if I want to.' The younger couple with her pulled ineffec-tually at her arm.

'No, you don't,' said Theo, walking her firmly out of the doorway and on to the drive. 'You didn't when the previous tenant held the lease, and you don't now. MovingInk have hired the manor. In any case it belongs to my father, not to you. I've got tea and coffee next door. I expect my cousins would like some after driving all the way over here.'

Out of the corner of my eye, I saw Coralie mentally step down from red alert to yellow. I got the feeling she only just didn't slam the door behind us to prevent re-entry.

'Jen, can you reach into my pocket for my keys?' said Theo, almost frogmarching his aunt between the houses.

'Sure,' I said, struck by an idea. 'Hold the lavender for me and I'll open up and get the kettle on. Hi, I'm Jen Matlock.'

Theo was so quick on the uptake. He angled himself so a waft of lavender scent drifted over his aunt as I reached into his pocket for the keys. Sadly, she appeared to be the one person in the world immune to its calming properties.

'You!' she said to me in a throbbing

voice. 'You're the herb woman.'

Her son — if it was her son — groaned.

'Yes, that's me.'

'My friend Felicity has bought stuff from you.'

It was said in tones of such loathing that I was taken aback. 'Oh dear. Was there a problem with the order? She should have said. I always refund if a customer is disappointed.' I got Theo's door open and headed for the kitchen. I definitely needed tea.

'No,' said Sue, surprisingly. 'Your remedies are always very good. Felicity and I swear by your seasickness tablets when we go on cruises.'

Cruises? No wonder she was in constant need of funds.

Theo really was fast. 'I'll just bet Felicity is on Jen's mailing list,' he said. He put the lavender on the table next to his aunt and leaned against the dresser, folding his arms across his chest.

'Exactly,' replied Sue in triumph.

I closed my eyes as the penny

dropped. My newsletter.

Which had gone out a couple of days ago.

With my new address on.

Which any great friend of Sue would be bound to know rather well.

'Coffee or tea?' I asked.

'Tea, please,' said the younger woman, who so far hadn't uttered a word. She rested a hand rather despairingly on her stomach and sank to a chair. 'Mint, for preference. No milk.'

Sue looked at her scornfully. 'Coffee,' she said to me. 'He's got a cafetiere. I gave it to his father six years ago for Christmas.'

I knew. We'd used it yesterday after dinner. I plugged my phone in at the wall as I waited for the kettle to boil. My email alert pinged with the link to Louise's diary I'd sent myself. I surreptitiously tapped it and nearly dropped the coffee packet as I read the website banner.

Manitoba History Collection, edited by Max Wright, Professor of Social

History, University of Winnipeg.

Manitoba? But surely Louise had emigrated to Australia. Why would her diary be in Manitoba? I tapped the diary transcript link.

'The point is, Theo,' said Sue, sounding quite reasonable. 'My solicitor tells me none of us are entitled to a percentage of the rent, now the original lease has finished.'

'Dad and I have both already explained that to you,' said Theo.

'We all have,' murmured her son.

'You didn't mention it until after you'd signed with the TV people though, did you?' she said to Theo with a flash of venom.

I poured boiling water into the cafetiere and the teapot, listening with half an ear, my eyes scurrying across the text on the phone screen.

Soon we will become Canadian citizens as part of the Empire Settlement programme.

It had been Canada they went to! Riffling back through my memory, I realised no one had ever specifically said Australia. I'd just assumed it. My eyes went to the top of the screen again. Professor Max Wright. Max. And a trickle of text I hadn't noticed before. *This diary forms part of the Wright family papers.*

'I'm extremely angry with you,' Sue was saying. 'I need that money. It's part of my income. I depend on it.' Her voice rose. 'And I'm going to see I get it.'

'There isn't any money,' said Theo wearily. 'The MovingInk hire is a short term deal. I need their fee just to keep Wansdale going.'

'Well, you won't get any more unless you cut me in.' She brandished a letter. 'You need three signatures for a change of use for all or part of the manor. I need the same to veto it. If I don't get any income, you don't either.'

Canada. Manitoba. Winnipeg.

Cousin John's boy, Max, at the university.

And the healing. Oh my God, the healing.

I rang Granny Annie, my phone still tethered to Theo's wall socket. 'Granny — two questions,' I said urgently, keeping a wary eye on the others, though I doubted Sue was listening to anyone but herself. 'Your grandma and grandpa. What were their Christian names? And their surname? And Cousin Max's surname, the one you said Ewan stayed with that time?'

Oh, God, it's true.

'In both those photos, your grandpa is leaning on a stick. Any reason?'

Oh heavens.

'One more question. Were our family always Canadian? Thanks, Granny. I can't talk now. I'll ring you later.'

I carried the tea and coffee to the table in a daze. Theo's aunt was thumping her fist on a letter, signed by three family members, refusing to let Wild About Herbs run a business from Wansdale Manor.

'Count them, Theo, three, just as the agreement states. Don't think I won't use this.'

Theo was looking harassed. A pulse of anger ran through me on his behalf. All he wanted was to be left in pace to run the manor. Almost certainly Anthony would be able to prove Sue's claim untenable, but . . .

I took a deep breath. 'You're wasting your time, I'm afraid. Theo's agreement with me predates yours.' I met his eyes and played my trump card. 'And it is signed by four members of the family.'

Theo's eyes widened.

Sue curled her lip. 'Nice try, dear, but you're wrong. I've checked with everyone. Theo hasn't even approached them. Your agreement can't possibly have been signed by more than him and my mother, since my brother is playing idiot tourist somewhere in the Mediterranean. I'm sorry for your business, dear, and I assure you that Felicity and I will still buy your products, but unless I get the cut owed to me, you're not going to be running it from Wansdale.'

'Yes I am,' I said. 'The agreement with Wild About Herbs is signed by four Wansdale family members. Theo, Barbara, my brother Chris and me. Louise Wright, nee Wansdale, was my great-great-grandma.'

18

It was considerably later. In the shocked silence after my announcement, I'd set up my laptop and Skyped Granny so that everyone could see her and hear her placidly confirm my deductions. Louise Wansdale had married Archie Wright in 1915. They had emigrated to Canada in 1923 with their daughter Dorothy and their sons Jack and Ian. Ian had begat John, who had begat Max, now a professor of social history and keeper of the Wright family papers. Dorothy had had two daughters, Laurel and Ann. Ann had married a Londoner and come to the UK at the beginning of the 1960s.

There were now so many more of us than there were of them, that Theo and his father could do anything they liked with Wansdale.

Faced with these unassailable facts,

Sue had ordered her son and daughter-in-law to take her home (but not before telling me she would expect a discount as a matter of course on anything she bought from Wild about Herbs in the future).

'I'm not convinced that four signatures does trump three, legally speaking,' said Theo once they'd gone.

'Nor me,' I said, 'but if I've learnt one thing from Mum over the years it's that if you say something reasonable in a firm enough tone, it always conveys authority. And our agreement did predate hers.'

Granny chuckled from the laptop.

'Have you got Max's email address?' I asked her. 'I'd love to know if there are any records of Louise between getting married and emigrating, while she and Archie were still here.' Although there probably weren't. New life, she'd said. She'd started afresh on the ship.

'I'll send it to you tomorrow, darling,' said Granny. 'Or you could ask Ewan. I'm late for bridge club and I'm dying to tell them the news.'

'Okay, have fun. I'll ask Dad to drive you up on his next day off. I can't wait to introduce you to Barbara. I think you'll get on.'

'I'd like that. It's not often you get to meet a long-lost cousin at my age. Bye, darling.'

'Bye Granny. Thank you again.' The screen went blank and I shut the lid.

'Barbara,' said Theo with a touch of guilt. 'I should tell her.'

'And I ought to tell Chris. Theo, one thing, and then I won't mention it again.'

'Go on.'

'Lady Mary was our joint great-great-great-grandmother. Does it make a difference?'

He smiled and shook his head. 'Not to me. Far too long ago. Two different branches. Five generations down the line. Does it matter to you?'

'Not in the least. I just thought I'd ask.'

Theo walked his fingers across the table to link with mine. 'Of course,' he said, 'we could *not* tell anyone for the moment, fetch an early meal from the catering truck and go to bed.'

'Best plan yet,' I said.

★　★　★

'I wonder if Louise simply forgot our diary?' I said to Theo next day as he watched me stripping feverfew into a drying tray. 'Looking at Granny's photos, she was evidently happy with Archie and I guess once the children came along she was too busy to dwell on the past. I hope Dorothy *was* Robbie's daughter, so she always had that memory, but she could easily have miscarried. I don't suppose we'll ever know now.'

'Oh, I think we will,' said Theo. 'I think we can be fairly sure already.'

He was grinning about something. 'What do you know that I don't?' I demanded. 'Have you been sneaking off to the family church to look through the baptismal register?'

'No, but that's a terrific idea. Actually, I remembered this,' he said. 'Exhibit A.'

He put a black and white photo on my workbench, evidently from the same set as the other photographs in Coralie's baskets. A Red Cross nurse and a soldier were standing awkwardly in front of my shed. The nurse wore a calf-length grey gown and a wide white headdress. She carried a trug with sheaves of lavender inside. The soldier had a pale complexion and freckles. He held a pair of shears and an armful of what looked like comfrey. 'Louise and Robbie,' I whispered.

'I think it has to be. Can you guess what Exhibit B is?' Alongside the photo he put a facsimile of one of the soldiers' letters that Bruce had used to flesh out the hospital scenes in the script.

I bent forward to read it. The writing was appalling, but the gist of the letter was that there had been great larks in the ward that day when Nurse Wansdale had had to slather poor old Ginger

Gibbs in lotion because he had a rash all over his body.

'They all had nicknames in those days,' said Theo. 'But there was usually only one reason a chap would be called Ginger.'

Ginger Gibbs. Robbie Gibbs. 'He must have had sandy hair,' I said. 'Like me. The chamomile was needed because he was allergic to rue. Also like me.'

'Red hair and sensitive skin. Straight down through Dorothy to you,' said Theo.

Robbie was my birth-ancestor. I groped for Theo's hand, my heart swelling as I gazed at the photo. Formal and posed as they were, he and Louise looked entirely right together. I didn't have words, so I said something trivial instead. 'I was right, there were no willows shading the shed then. Look, there's a corner of your wall and one of the beehives.'

'So there is.'

Beehives . . . Wall . . . Herbs . . .

'Bees!' I yelled. 'Theo, it's the bees!' Glorious understanding burst upon me, layer upon layer of it, all falling like gossamer sheets and melding together into a perfect whole. I clutched both his hands and swung around to face him.

'What's the bees?' he asked.

I gave his hands a shake. 'The answer! *Wansdale land holds Wansdale bounty, richest prize in all the county, thyme on dial leads arrow-straight, through the wall and o'er the gate.*'

'I know the rhyme,' he said drily.

'But the answer to it is right there! And it *is* a rhyme, not a riddle, because they knew the answer all along.'

'Jen, I have no idea what you are talking about.'

'Thyme! Remember what John Goode said in Rev Septimus's account? *The monks' honey is accounted most superior and mends all manner of bodily injuries as well as being the finest I ever tasted.* Theo, honey has been used for centuries to bind wounds. Thyme is an antiseptic. Thyme honey is almost the most flavourful there is. In an era without modern medicine, it would have been priceless! There are hundreds of different varieties of thyme — suppose one of them is indigenous to Wansdale? That's why the planting plan doesn't matter. The thyme would always be on the herb dial somewhere. And the bees would harvest the nectar and fly straight from the plants, through the pierced openings on your walled garden and over the gate to the hives!'

He stared at me. 'Honey? That's it? That's the Wansdale Bounty? You mean I climbed the stable clock and got myself spitted for nothing?'

I brought his hands to my lips and kissed them, still buoyed up by having solved the rhyme. 'You already knew that. Theo, this could be important. We have to see if anywhere in this garden is the original Wansdale thyme. After all, rosemary and sage and lavender are still here. The wintergreen was still holding its own under the willows. Some of the thyme plants might also have escaped the tenants' wholesale makeover, don't you think? Some tiny, scrappy, sunny, forgotten patch? I swear I haven't dug any up. The only thyme plants I've seen here are garden thyme. I know it isn't very likely, but oh it would *so* be something if we located any.'

Theo was looking rather sick at the answer to the riddle not being material treasure that he could sell to plough back into the estate.

I let go of his hands. 'If we do find a patch, I can propagate it. Then we could get a premium return on the honey,' I said, trying to soften the blow. 'We could call it *Wansdale Bounty*. Think how much Manuka honey sells for.'

He sighed. 'I always knew the idea of treasure was too good to be true. Back to the hard work, no privacy and years of poverty option. How about if I try the plant bank at Kew? That's where I got some of the heritage vegetables that I grow.'

I beamed at him. 'Worth a try. Meanwhile I'll go over the whole garden centimetre by centimetre. Louise was using Wansdale honey on the soldiers' wounds so there is just a chance the thyme is still here. Herbs can cling on in forgotten pockets almost indefinitely. I'll start by tracking the bees backwards. They adore thyme flowers. They found the bushes I planted in the herb dial as soon as they were in the ground.'

Theo got up, took a few steps, then frowned. 'Wait,' he said slowly. 'Track the bees . . .'

As I watched, his face perceptibly drained of colour.

'What's the matter?' I asked, taking his elbow.

'Bees.' He spoke jerkily. 'On the old stable clock. One of the things that startled me. I'd forgotten. There's a small recess. A triangular pocket where some turrets form an inner corner. Soil has built up there. Woody, tiny-leaved plants. Pungent when I trod on it. There were bees all over it.'

I gripped his arm, my heart hammering. 'Wansdale thyme,' I breathed, 'though I'm not sure how we'd know it, apart from by eliminating all the other varieties. Can we reach the recess from inside?'

'Not a chance. The windows are too small. I'll get the ladder.'

But still he hesitated, and suddenly I knew why. I had felt the wrongness in his body the first moment I'd laid eyes on his scar. I'd run mental hands over the barrier that he'd slammed around his fall. He'd imprisoned his failure. I'd provided a key. And he wanted out.

He cleared his throat. 'Or I could climb,' he said.

Fear stole an icy hand around my heart. 'Or you could climb.'

He stood straighter, gazing neutrally into the middle distance. 'I'd better change my shoes.'

Dear God, he was going to do it. Just like that. And I found it was one thing to blithely identify the cause of his problem and quite another thing to stand calmly by and watch the man I loved make another attempt to do something that had damn near killed him seven years ago.

'Theo . . . '

You've given me back my life.

That's what he'd said, but it hadn't been true. To give it back, I had to give it back completely.

He turned his head, a tiny, don't-go-there challenge in his eyes. I swallowed. 'Take care, right? Because I don't know your dad nearly as well as I know you and I don't think the rest of your relations are very keen on me running my business from here.'

They were the right words. He grinned. 'No problem. I just have to climb with my heart, not my head. How hard can it be?'

I watched the door close behind him, then with numb, frantic fingers I fumbled my phone out of my pocket and hit my brother Chris's speed dial. 'Theo is going to climb the stable block,' I gabbled. 'It's where he fell before. And it's absolutely right, but it's also my fault. And . . . and I could do with another night climber here to . . . to congratulate him when he's done

349

it.' I gulped. 'And . . . and maybe to act as backup.'

Chris swore softly. 'On my way. Sorry guys, emergency.' The line went dead.

I managed to delay Theo a few minutes at the bottom of the building by fussing around handing him polythene bags for samples. Just as I was out of time I heard the screech of Chris's tyres on the gravel of the dower house drive.

'Nice day for a scramble,' said my brother, strolling across. He looked up at the stable block with an appraising eye.

Theo gave me a long, long look. Then he bent his head and kissed me full on the lips. 'I love you too,' he said.

And with a brief run up and a casual hand on the drainpipe, he was gone.

★   ★   ★

It was, without a doubt, the very worst fifteen minutes of my life. Theo had no ropes, no special equipment, just grippy shoes and the knowledge in his hands that he had climbed hundreds of buildings with his heart and his instinct and not come to harm.

Alerted by Chris's arrival, the crew were already filming. What was Theo doing? Why was he doing it?

'If we'd known,' said Bruce reproachfully, 'we could have miked him up.'

'Bruce!' said Coralie. Her hand edged into Chris's.

I answered all the questions haphazardly, not taking my eyes off Theo for one moment. I could see his ascent was clever, fluid, a thing of beauty, but all the time my mind was screaming *What if? What if? What if?*

He had reached the turrets, swung himself up to the first ledge. Beside me, Chris murmured encouragement. Theo disappeared from view and I swear all of us held our breath. There was the tiny skitter of a stone or a fragment of masonry. Then he reappeared another half level up. He edged himself around one corner, around a second. There was a tiny check, a hesitation. This was the danger point, I could sense it: this was where he'd fallen last time. He went on. Someone made an anxious sound and I realised it was me.

He stooped, his voice coming down indistinctly.

'What's he doing?' said Coralie.

I fought down the beginnings of hysteria. 'I don't believe this. He's talking to the bees.'

Theo glanced down at me and raised his thumb to show he'd found the thyme.

He crouched awkwardly, taking cuttings and hopefully teasing out a piece with roots attached, then tucked the bags into his pocket and swung down to the ridge of the roof below.

I closed my eyes. 'Is it over yet?' I asked Chris.

'Ask him yourself,' said my brother. 'Here he is.'

'Wansdale thyme,' said Theo, presenting me with a clutch of polythene bags.

The casual tone of his voice didn't

fool me one little bit. I turned blindly and held him as if I would never let him go.

⋆   ⋆   ⋆

Bruce went back to his filming. Chris regretfully went back to work. I hurried the tiny pieces of thyme into my propagator and told them fiercely and lovingly that they had better live and thrive and grow beautiful because I would age by another hundred years myself if Theo had to do that climb again.

I turned to find him leaning against the door jamb and laughing at me. 'I suppose that disposes of the question of whether you only want me for my garden,' he said.

'Dammit, Theo, how unfair are you! I had an answer all ready for when you asked me that. I was going to suck my breath in and go 'We-e-e-ell ... ' How can I do that today?'

He walked over and put his arms

around me. 'Too soft by half.'

'There's a way not to be? Theo, that was terrifying. I'm glad you did it, for you, but all the time you were up there, I was wishing you weren't.'

He held me close. 'I love you, Jen.'

He'd said it. He'd committed himself. Everything in me melted and reformed.

'I love you too,' I said.

Then I raised my head and our lips met and we claimed each other, both of us equal, two parts of a whole.

Acknowledgements

Any mistakes are my own, but I owe thanks to

The Geffrye Museum for their wonderful herb and period gardens

Elizabeth Chadwick for pointers to medieval wound management

Tara Lee Platt for allowing me to borrow her accident (it's okay, she's fine now)

Lesley Lamont Fisher for being endlessly knowledgeable about the making of TV drama documentaries

and you, if I've forgotten to include you

We do hope that you have enjoyed reading this large print book.

Did you know that all of our titles are available for purchase?

We publish a wide range of high quality large print books including:
**Romances, Mysteries, Classics
General Fiction
Non Fiction and Westerns**

Special interest titles available in large print are:
**The Little Oxford Dictionary
Music Book, Song Book
Hymn Book, Service Book**

Also available from us courtesy of Oxford University Press:
**Young Readers' Dictionary
(large print edition)
Young Readers' Thesaurus
(large print edition)**

For further information or a free brochure, please contact us at:
**Ulverscroft Large Print Books Ltd.,
The Green, Bradgate Road, Anstey,
Leicester, LE7 7FU, England.
Tel:** (00 44) **0116 236 4325
Fax:** (00 44) **0116 234 0205**

LOVE WILL FIND A WAY

Miranda Barnes

Convalescing after a car accident, Gwen Yorke leases a remote cottage on the beautiful Isle of Skye. She hopes to find inspiration there for her career as a rug designer, and wants to decide if she and her boyfriend have a future together. In Glenbrittle, she finds herself drawn to the enigmatic, moody Andrew McIver, and his young daughter Fiona. To Gwen's delight, she and Fiona become close, frequently sketching together. But why is Andrew so unhappy about their friendship?

THE PRINCE'S BRIDE

Sophie Weston

One of three royal brothers in the Adriatic principality of San Michele, Prince Jonas works hard. But after a protocol-ridden evening, he's due some downtime in his beloved forest. Hope Kennard was the daughter of the manor back in England. But she has guarded her heart since her childhood ended in financial scandal. She's just passing through San Michele, before moving on to another country, another job. But then a charming forest ranger appears. And this time, her instincts don't help . . .

THE UNEXPECTED GIFT

Sarah Purdue

When London nurse Megan Falstaff is informed she's received an inheritance from her beloved godmother Cathleen, she's expecting a couple of cat figurines. What she actually inherits is a boarding cattery in the village of Little River — with the stipulation that she must run it for at least a year. Getting to grips with the eccentricities of felines and village folk alike is challenging for Megan — and matters aren't helped by the disdain of the haughty vet Doctor William Wakefield . . .

ONLY TRUE IN FAIRY TALES

Christine Stovell

Eloise Blake has been fascinated by Prospect House, the shadowy romantic Gothic edifice opposite hers, ever since she moved to the village of Hookfield. When its new owner turns out to be bestselling crime author Ross Farrell, whose work is grounded in gritty reality rather than happy endings, she is determined to concentrate on her tapestry design business and her rescue dog Gracie. Love, she thinks, is only true in fairy tales. But is Ross the Prince Charming she thought didn't exist — or is he a beast in disguise?